Rumors were flying at [...] Cattleman's Club last night when Zach Dumas walked in with Leslie Hall, the gorgeous—and controversial—E.R. doctor from West View Hospital. Heads turned and an audible buzz followed the popular rancher as he led his date to a secluded table in the opulent dining room.

It's not unusual to see Dumas at the club, though the divorced father of two is more at home rounding up cattle on his successful Twin Bar Ranch outside Reno. But club patrons had to be a little surprised at his choice of companion.

Review reporters have discovered that Dr. Hall left her previous position at a California hospital under questionable circumstances and has been assigned a longer than usual probation period at West View.

requests for an interview, which makes us wonder—what exactly are they trying to hide?

One thing is certain. Judging by the way the handsome couple were snuggling on the dance floor, the mystery swirling around Dr. Hall doesn't bother Zach Dumas one little bit. The Reno rancher obviously likes his romance with a shot of intrigue.

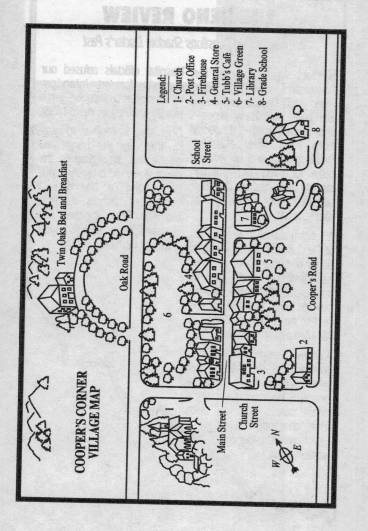

COOPER'S CORNER
VILLAGE MAP

Twin Oaks Bed and Breakfast

Oak Road

Main Street

Church Street

Cooper's Road

School Street

Legend:
1- Church
2- Post Office
3- Firehouse
4- General Store
5- Tubb's Café
6- Village Green
7- Library
8- Grade School

W • N • E
S

COOPER'S CORNER

JESSICA MATTHEWS

The Search

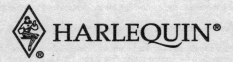

HARLEQUIN®

TORONTO • NEW YORK • LONDON
AMSTERDAM • PARIS • SYDNEY • HAMBURG
STOCKHOLM • ATHENS • TOKYO • MILAN • MADRID
PRAGUE • WARSAW • BUDAPEST • AUCKLAND

HARLEQUIN BOOKS
225 Duncan Mill Road, Don Mills,
Ontario, Canada M3B 3K9

ISBN 0-373-61264-8

THE SEARCH

Jessica Matthews is acknowledged as the author of this work.

Visit us at www.eHarlequin.com

Printed in U.S.A.

Dear Reader,

I'm so delighted to be a part of the Cooper's Corner continuity series. *The Search* begins the story of the western branch of the Cooper family and is dear to my heart because it reminds me of my own experiences with genealogical research. As everyone who's ever embarked on such a quest knows, uncovering the past is challenging, exciting and disappointing at times. However, in the end, every piece of history becomes a nugget of gold. Just as my own curiosity compelled me to keep going, Zach's curiosity won't allow him to give up, even though he travels down a path where he finds more questions than answers.

I hope Zach's story will touch your heart as he finds much more than he bargained for on his journey of discovery— an enduring love.

Best wishes and happy reading!

Jessica Matthews
www.jessicamatthews.com

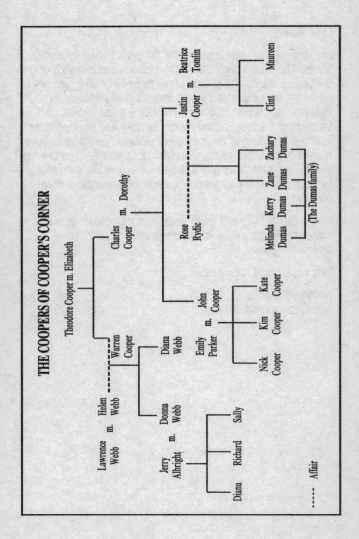

THE COOPERS OF COOPER'S CORNER

Theodore Cooper m. Elizabeth

Lawrence Webb m. Helen Webb

Warren Cooper — Diana Webb

Donna Webb

Jerry Albright m.

Diana   Richard   Sally

Charles Cooper m. Dorothy

John Cooper — Emily Parker

Nick Cooper   Kim Cooper   Kate Cooper

Rose Rydic

Justin Cooper m. Beatrice Tomlin

Clint   Maureen

Melinda Dumas   Kerry Dumas   Zane Dumas   Zachary Dumas

(The Dumas family)

----- Affair

PROLOGUE

Early '60s

"HEY, COOP. We're going out to celebrate. Are you coming with us or not?"

Seated on the lumpy sofa in front of the television set with his feet propped on the cluttered coffee table, Justin Cooper watched the opening credits of a Civil War documentary.

"Go ahead," he told his roommate as he mentally noted the Georgia location where the filming had occurred. "I'll join you after this is over."

Bradley snorted, then moved closer to Justin. "Like I believe you, Coop," he scoffed. "I know exactly what will happen. You'll watch this program, and before it's over, you'll drag out your dusty books to verify the information in it."

Justin glanced in his friend's direction, and a lock of hair fell into his eyes. Out of habit, he brushed it back and vowed to take time for a haircut now that his midterms were over and he could think about something other than memorizing names, dates and political ideologies.

"No, I won't," he said, although he knew his friend had pegged him correctly. He'd known Bradley since their undergraduate days, and in the intervening years, his friend had learned most, if not all, of Justin's idiosyncrasies. Justin didn't particularly mind. He knew Bradley's flaws as well as his own, which gave their friendship a remarkable system of checks and balances.

"You will, too," Bradley insisted. "You do it every time. I have witnesses who will back me one hundred percent."

"Since when is it a crime to get caught up in a television program?" Justin argued in his usual mild manner.

"It's not, but last I knew, no one's appointed you as the American history watchdog," Bradley countered. "Come on. We aced our exams and now it's time to cut loose and celebrate. I hear the Harbor Lounge has some new talent." He wiggled his eyebrows.

Justin gave him a long-suffering glance. "I'm not interested in being a third wheel. *Again,* I might add."

"This time it will be different," Bradley cajoled. "We're meeting Richard, Carl and Perry, so if I find a little female companionship—" he winked "—you won't be alone."

Justin sighed. After hours of cramming with nothing but coffee in his belly, he wanted a quiet evening at home to unwind. "I can celebrate here. I've got a six-pack of beer and a bag of pretzels."

Bradley shook his head. "Not good enough. Tell you what. Just hang around with us for a couple of hours. I'll even buy the first round."

Justin raised one dark eyebrow. It wasn't as if he didn't have the money for a couple of drinks. He'd simply rather spend it on something more worthwhile than courting a hangover. Still, if the tightfisted Bradley was willing to shell out a few bucks...

He glanced at the television screen while trying to decide—watching a documentary in peace and quiet versus sitting in a smoke-filled, noisy room where you couldn't hear yourself think. Geez, what a choice.

"Come on, Coop," Bradley wheedled. "At least stay for an hour. You know what they say. All work and no play makes Justin a dull boy."

The word *dull* hit a sore spot, and he winced. He'd always preferred poring over history books and poking around historical sites to the more physical challenges of sports. As a result he'd been teased mercilessly by the school jocks and looked down upon by the girls. To compensate, he'd learned to sail, but his preference to take his boat out on the water alone in order to hear the seagulls and the waves lapping against the hull hadn't done much to change their opinion.

"Kick up your heels for once," Bradley continued. "People in your history books *did* something besides sit at home and watch the grass grow. Otherwise, they wouldn't be mentioned at all."

Bradley had a point. Sixteen-year-old Bobby Fischer wouldn't have successfully defended the U.S. chess title, Arnold Palmer wouldn't have won the U.S. Open golf championship and R. C. Webster wouldn't have landed a 410-pound blue shark off the coast of Massachusetts if they'd stayed at home.

Maybe he *should* go. Granted, an evening at the Harbor Lounge didn't compare to a historic chess or golf tournament, but agreeing to this excursion would stop Bradley's wheedling. Until the next time, that is.

After casting one last longing glance at the black-and-white screen, he rose and walked over to turn the set off. The picture faded to dark. "All right," he said. "One hour."

"You won't be sorry," Bradley promised, apparently satisfied by his limited victory.

"I hope not."

His wish came true thirty minutes later. As Justin slid into the booth at the Harbor Lounge, the sight of the beautiful, tawny-haired woman who appeared on stage immediately caught his attention. He craned his neck for a better view over the full house as she glided toward the microphone. Anticipation hummed through his veins. If her graceful movements weren't enough to stir his blood, her sultry voice was as she said hello to the crowd.

He shifted his wire-rimmed spectacles to clear his vision. She was perfection personified. Her slim-fitting cocktail dress sparkled under the stage lights as it hugged generous curves. Her features were stunning, and even from this distance, he could see skin as velvety soft as a rose. No doubt she'd smell as good as one, too.

Justin wanted her to turn her sexy smile and come-hither eyes in his direction more than he'd ever wanted anything before in his life. A moment later, she did, and his thoughts instantly turned to ways he could arrange for an introduction with this golden-haired beauty.

She began to sing, and he listened, mesmerized. He knew enough about music to recognize that she possessed more talent than most. Every note she hit came out pure and on perfect pitch. She was a genuine songbird.

At the end of her first number, the crowd erupted into whistles and applause. He nudged Bradley and raised his voice over the din. "Who is she?"

"Rose Rydic. She's hot, isn't she?"

Hot didn't describe her adequately in Justin's opinion. Impulsively, he beckoned a nearby cocktail waitress. "Can I borrow your pen for a minute?" Without waiting for her reply, he snatched it off her tray and began scribbling on a napkin.

"Hey," the young woman protested. "You can't do that. I need it."

"I'll give it back. Just a second." Justin completed his customary scrawl, in the end, his excitement made it as illegible as usual. He placed the note on her order pad. "Would you give this to Miss Rydic, please?"

The redhead frowned. "Do I look like a messenger service, bub?"

Justin pulled a ten-dollar bill out of his pocket. As a tip, it was far too generous, but he considered the amount an investment. He laid it on top of the napkin. "You look like a girl who deserves a little extra for her efforts."

The redhead's eyes nearly bugged out of her head. "Okay, but don't expect an answer. Rose doesn't mingle with the customers."

"Just give her the note."

She quickly slipped the bill into the pocket of her short black skirt. "It's your money. Don't say I didn't warn you, though."

"I won't." He sat back to wait as the woman meandered past the crowded tables to reach Rose.

Bradley's eyes widened. "Hey, old buddy. Did you do what I think you just did?"

Suddenly tense over the outcome, Justin took a long drag on his beer. "Yeah."

Bradley and the rest of his friends hooted. "I never thought I'd live to see the day when Justin Cooper was interested in anything or anyone less than a hundred years old."

"Yeah, well, now you have." Justin's gaze followed the redhead's progress through the crowd, and he watched her pass the message to Rose. She glanced at him, and he fought a sudden urge to remove his wire-rimmed glasses in order to lessen his scholarly appearance. It was too late for that, however, so instead, he smiled.

Without changing her pleasant expression, Rose spoke in the waitress's ear. A few seconds later, the redhead nodded, then headed in his direction while Rose began another song.

Every muscle in his body seemed to freeze in anticipation, and he nearly groaned aloud as a large group at another table sidetracked the waitress to order another round.

Justin drummed his fingers on the scarred surface, irritated by the delay. Surely she would accept his invitation. He might not have Bradley's Adonis-blond looks, but his face didn't give people nightmares. If Rose refused to meet him later, he'd simply find another way to talk to her. It might take time, but he would not fail—even if he had to camp here every evening for the rest of the fall semester.

The redhead came close. "She'll be at the back door at midnight. Don't be late."

He nearly laughed aloud. Nothing would keep him from this appointment. Instead, he exhaled the breath he'd been holding and flashed her a wide grin. "Thanks."

Bradley clapped his hand on Justin's back. "You lucky dog. Who would have figured she'd go for the studious type? Aren't you glad you came?" He spoke to the whole group. "I think our old buddy Justin is about to make some history of his own."

Justin shrugged nonchalantly at his friends' teasing, but inside he was as eager as an archeologist who'd stumbled across a rare find. His instincts were already whispering that Rose was the special woman he'd been waiting for all of his life.

Midnight was still a few hours away, but he couldn't think of a better way to pass the time than to watch Rose's performance and dream of the future.

CHAPTER ONE

Present day

WHAT IN BLAZES was taking so long?

Zachary Dumas paced the floor of the waiting area outside West View Hospital's emergency room. He hadn't felt this helpless since his father's heart attack several years ago, and as a man accustomed to making decisions and giving orders, he didn't like this feeling one bit.

He was out of his element here. A veterinary office was more his style, and clearly, from the looks he'd received from the other people in the waiting room, they agreed. Everyone had given him a wide berth, but whether it was due to his disreputable appearance or the fact he was acting as nervous as a long-tailed cat in a room full of rocking chairs, he didn't know and didn't care.

He clutched the brim of his brown Stetson with one hand and wiped his forehead on his long sleeve. After his sister Melinda's divorce from that weasel Orly Haas, she and her two children had moved in with their widowed brother, Zane, who was also Zach's twin. With Zane in South America and their parents, Eleanor and Hamilton, in Arizona on vacation, the reins of responsibility for the Dumas family and their holdings had fallen to Zach.

Right now, that responsibility weighed heavily on his shoulders.

Zane's ranch manager had located him in the southeast corner of his half of the Twin Bar Ranch and informed him of Melinda's accident. Immediately Zach had ridden his Appaloosa to ranch headquarters, tossed the reins to one of his hands, rinsed the trail dust off his face, then jumped into his truck and broken the speed limit on his way to the hospital.

He smelled of horse and sweat and dirt—odors that contrasted mightily with the aroma of disinfectant that surrounded him. Perhaps he should have taken a few minutes to shower before he drove to town, but once he'd heard the word *serious,* he hadn't been inclined to waste time. He couldn't be the first fellow who'd ever arrived in the emergency room wearing a sweat-stained shirt, well-worn jeans and scuffed boots, and he'd lay down money that he wouldn't be the last.

He glanced at the clock, and his impatience grew like wild mushrooms after a spring rain. The old gal at the desk—a thin, middle-aged woman who ate crab apples for lunch, if her expression was any indication—had mentioned that the doctor would talk to him as soon as possible. Unfortunately, as soon as possible had already stretched into fifty minutes. If he figured in the hour Zane's manager had needed to find him and the thirty-minute trip to reach West View, Melinda had been closeted in the ER for nearly three hours.

It couldn't be good news. He'd seen enough episodes of the television show *ER* and witnessed more than his share of trail mishaps to imagine the worst. Melinda was an experienced horsewoman, but any number of reasons could account for why she'd fallen off one of Zane's Arabian mares. She'd gone through a lot in the past year with her divorce, and because he'd been there, done that, he understood how preoccupied she might have been. Accidents happened even to the most cautious of folk.

Eager to do something, *anything,* Zach slapped his hat against his leg and sent a cloud of dust into the air. The persimmon-faced lady at the desk cleared her throat and frowned. He almost felt guilty, then was tempted to repeat his actions, if for no other reason than to irritate the woman. If she didn't want him dirtying the place, she could light a fire under the doctor so he'd update Zach on Melinda's condition.

He'd barely finished his thought before the right side of the double doors swung open. A woman in her midthirties, clad in a white coat with a stethoscope around her neck, hesitated in the opening while she scanned the crowd.

Her intense, dark-eyed gaze landed on him, then lingered. He felt an instant connection, as if they were both tuned into the same frequency. While she didn't have the cover model looks of his ex-wife, she was one attractive lady in Zach's books. Her reddish-brown hair reminded him of the rich hue of the old mahogany rolltop desk he'd bought at an estate auction and appeared just as smooth as its polished surface.

Her lab coat hung limply over shapeless blue scrubs, and her expression reflected her weariness. From the standing-room-only status of the waiting area, he assumed her obvious exhaustion was the result of a long, hard day, if not one of many.

Suddenly, the questioning wrinkle on her forehead disappeared, and she strode purposefully toward him. Like any man who'd been singled out, he went on alert. The absence of a reassuring smile warned him of im-

pending bad news, and his gut churned. He squared his
shoulders and braced himself, aware that his breath
seemed to catch in his throat.

"Mr. Dumas?" she asked.

"That's me. How's my sister?"

She held out her hand and met his gaze. "I'm Dr.
Hall."

Although she appeared coolly professional—clearly
she wasn't a woman who engaged in polite chitchat—
a sense of calm shone out of her walnut-brown eyes,
which Zach took as a good sign. He clasped her hand,
pleased that her grip was firm in spite of her fine bone
structure. He could tell a lot about a person from the
way they shook hands and looked him in the eye. Dr.
Leslie Hall, according to the name embroidered in red
thread above her left breast pocket, had passed his test
with flying colors. She might appear fragile, but he suspected that pure steel formed her backbone.

"How's my sister?" he repeated.

She led him toward a corner where they had a mod-
icum of privacy. "Melinda is in serious condition," she
began.

"How serious?"

"Her arm is broken in several places."

Sweet relief flooded over him. "That's all?" Hell,
he'd broken his arm several years ago when one of his
steers had gotten cantankerous and knocked him against
a split rail fence. A few X rays, a cast for six weeks,
and he was good as new. Of course, he could forecast
a weather change by the resultant ache, but sometimes
his ability was more blessing than curse.

"It's more complicated than that," she said in a voice
that was as soothing as the sound of the spring-fed

stream that trickled down a rocky slope to feed his stock pond.

Worry started to replace his relief. "Oh?"

"Melinda has what we call an open or a compound fracture, which means that broken pieces of bone have punched through the skin. Some of those pieces were crushed, and she's showing signs of radial nerve damage and decreased circulation. I've called in an orthopedic surgeon, and he plans to operate to repair the damage."

"Fine," he said impatiently. "When will he fix her arm? Now?"

Dr. Hall shook her head. "I'm afraid it will be a while."

"I thought you said she has decreased circulation and radial nerve damage. Don't you need to correct the problem right away?"

"Relatively speaking, yes, we do," she admitted. "The delay is because we've found a problem with Melinda's preop lab work."

"Problem?" Zach hardened his voice. "What sort of problem?"

"We normally ask for a few units of compatible blood to be on hand for patients with this type of surgery. Unfortunately, our blood bank hasn't been able to accommodate our request."

"Why not?"

"Melinda has a rare antibody in her blood that's making it difficult to find suitable matches for her."

"How did *that* happen?" he asked.

"According to what she's told me, she received a transfusion after her youngest child was born. Apparently the unit of blood contained a blood group protein that her body recognized as foreign. As a result, her immune system reacted by producing an antibody to destroy it.''

''So what do we do?''

''We find blood that doesn't contain the corresponding protein antigen. Otherwise, she'll suffer a reaction and die,'' Dr. Hall said bluntly.

For a moment, he was speechless.

''We have the regional blood center in Reno searching for units, and if they can't find any, they'll contact the National Rare Donor Registry.''

''How long will that take?''

She shrugged. ''It could take hours and it could take days. It just depends.''

He focused on the one word. ''Days? You'll wait *days* to perform my sister's surgery? I thought you said she had a circulation problem.'' He knew enough about medicine to know that you didn't wait indefinitely to restore blood flow.

''We won't wait that long,'' she assured him. ''It's unlikely that we'll transfuse her at all, but Dr. Stone wants to play it safe. He's willing to wait a few hours to give the blood bank staff an opportunity to find compatible units. However, if Melinda's condition deteriorates, he'll proceed with the surgery.''

Hating to see his sister wait when he could potentially solve the problem, he said, ''I'm her brother. Use my blood.''

A faint smile tugged at her mouth. ''It's not that simple. Our FDA regulations don't allow us to draw donors. The amount of testing required is phenomenal, and we simply aren't equipped to handle it. However, to cover our bases, we could check your blood type to see if you are a match for your sister. If so, we'll send you across town to the Red Cross donor center.''

"Let's do it." As much as he hated being on the receiving end of a needle, he'd walk barefoot on burning coals for Melinda. For that matter, he'd do the same for anyone in his family, including his twin, Zane, wherever he might be these days.

Admit it, his conscience argued. *You just want to hang around the lovely Dr. Leslie Hall.*

True, he mentally conceded. It had been six months or more since he'd felt like asking a woman out, and although Leslie Hall hadn't sent any signals indicating a mutual attraction, something about her drew him to her. As a man who'd suffered his share of heartfelt pain, he recognized the shadows in her eyes and wanted to chase them away, even if only for a few hours. No doubt she had seen more senseless tragedy in her profession than most people would see in several lifetimes, but it seemed even more tragic to know it had marked her, albeit in a subtle way. Maybe when Melinda was back in the proverbial saddle, he could call Leslie and they could swap stories.

"If you'll come with me, I'll draw your blood sample and send it directly to the lab to save time," she said, leading him to the double doors. "After we're done, you can see your sister."

She led him to her tiny office off the nurses' station and called the lab to explain what she wanted. Zach listened shamelessly as she coaxed the technologist to do this special favor for her. One thing was sure. If she asked him to do anything in that tone of voice, he wouldn't think twice before he agreed.

A few minutes later, Zach rolled up his sleeve while she assembled her supplies, but before she tied the tourniquet around his arm, he drew back.

"You'll let me know the results right away?" he asked.

"Absolutely."

"How long will it take?"

"Thirty or forty minutes."

"Okay." He extended his arm and noticed her fresh garden-flower scent as she bent over him. Suddenly, he felt self-conscious about his appearance. Eau-de-horse wasn't a fragrance on cologne counters and certainly wouldn't impress the lady. Someday, he vowed, he'd show her just how well he cleaned up.

To his surprise and great relief, the process was painless. After she'd filled several colored vials, it was over. Strangely enough, he was reluctant to leave her presence, although she hadn't said a word.

"Does this happen often?" he asked.

"Does what happen often?" she returned as she printed his name on the tubes.

"Not being able to find blood for a person."

"No. Our American Red Cross donor facility works miracles."

"Let's hope they can pull one out of their hat for my sister."

"Even if they can't, we have a few other options, so don't worry. We won't compromise Melinda's health."

Zach met her brown-eyed gaze and held it. "Does that promise come with a guarantee?"

The corners of her mouth twitched as if she could have smiled but for some reason wouldn't. "We don't give guarantees in the medical profession. However, Dr. Stone is the best orthopedic surgeon on staff. I have the utmost confidence in him."

"I guess that will have to do, won't it?"

"I'm afraid so. Would you like to sit with your sister?"

Zach unrolled his sleeve and buttoned the cuff. "Please."

Dr. Hall pointed in a southerly direction. "She's in room six."

Zach followed the doctor to Melinda's room, wondering if the physician treated everyone with such businesslike precision. As they passed the staff in the hallway, everyone greeted her with deference, but Zach never saw her expression change or her face break into a full smile. He could understand her detached manner with patients, but it seemed unusual to treat her co-workers and colleagues the same way.

"Busy place," he commented.

"It usually is," she said politely. Pausing outside the door labeled with a huge number six, she knocked, then pushed it open. "You have a visitor, Melinda."

Zach hid his surprise at Melinda's pallor, which seemed more pronounced than usual. Her brown hair lay limply against the pillow, and lines of pain appeared on her face. Her eyes were red-rimmed and they brimmed with tears as she recognized him. The best thing to do as far as he could tell was to take his sister's mind off her injury. Facing a crying woman was as nerve-racking as facing an irritable bull—a man didn't know what either one would do next.

"Hey there, sis. How's the room service around here?"

She swiped at her eyes and giggled, which was what he'd intended. He leaned over and kissed her forehead. "How are you feeling?"

"Better, now that I know you're here."

"Wild horses—in my case, ornery cows—couldn't

keep me away," he teased. "Although if you wanted some R and R, Mel, you could have chosen something more exotic than West View Hospital."

Melinda smiled, although Zach saw the shimmer of moisture in her eyes. "What can I say? It was close to home." She sighed. "Heaven only knows it won't be cheap."

Certain she would fret over her finances if given the opportunity, he changed the subject. "The main thing is for you to get back in tip-top condition. It sounds as if you have some good doctors on your case." Although he focused his attention on his sister, he was extremely aware of Dr. Hall's presence as she examined Melinda's fingers and took her pulse. Her face remained impassive, not giving him a clue as to what she'd found. He chose to think positively.

"Everyone's been wonderful," Melinda answered.

"Are you in any pain?" he asked.

She shrugged. "My arm throbs a little. The pill they gave me worked wonders."

Dr. Hall interrupted. "I'll be back to check on you shortly. If you need anything, push the call button."

As soon as she closed the door behind her, Zach faced Melinda. "Want to tell me what happened?"

Melinda's chin quivered, and her soft brown eyes filled with tears again. "I was on my way back to the house, dreaming up plans to expand my limousine service. All of a sudden, I'm flying through the air. Naturally, my horse picked a spot close to a huge boulder to decide he was scared of a ground squirrel. When I landed, I heard the bone snap and, well, you know the rest."

He patted her shoulder. "Don't worry. You'll be fixed in no time."

She shook her head. "No, I won't. This is going to kill my business for at least six to eight weeks. How in the world am I going to pay for all this?" She gestured with her good arm.

"That's what insurance is for."

"It would be if I *had* health insurance." She sniffled. "But I don't. I can't afford the premiums, and Orly's scumbag lawyer fixed it so Orly doesn't have to pay one red cent for Nancy and Ryan's coverage, either. I'm already in debt to my eyebrows. This little episode is going to cost *thousands* of dollars that I don't have and don't have any way to earn." Her voice rose.

"Calm down, Mel," Zach said, wishing he could meet Orly in a dark alley and mete out his own brand of justice. Then he'd like to do the same to his snake-hearted, shyster attorney. "You know the family will help you."

Melinda burst into tears. "That's the problem," she sobbed. "I'm always depending on you. Every time I think things are turning around and it looks as if I'll finally stand on my own two feet, something awful happens, and I end up where I was before. A charity case."

Zach sat on the edge of her bed near her good arm and drew her close. "You are not a charity case. You're family, and we're supposed to help each other out. Besides, this bad spell won't last forever. You'll repay the favor when you can. Who knows? I may fall into dire straits someday, and only a gorgeous limo driver will be able to help me."

She chuckled, which was the reaction Zach wanted. He handed her a tissue, and after she blew her nose and dried her eyes, she smiled. "You always know the right things to say, don't you?"

Privately, he disagreed. If he'd said the right things

to his wife, Monica, he might have avoided his divorce. Still, if Melinda thought he was wonderful, he wasn't going to argue with her. A man needed to have his ego stroked every now and then, and his account in that department was currently overdrawn. "I try," he hedged.

She mopped her face with a corner of the sheet. "What about Nancy and Ryan? Did you find them?"

"Kerry did," he said, referring to their cousin. After Kerry's parents died on a geological trip in Nevada's desert when she was five, Zach's parents had adopted her. But Kerry fit into their family so well that Zach thought of her more as his sister than his cousin, and often referred to her that way.

"Doesn't she have to be at work?"

"She can take a day or two off. By now, she's probably picked up the kids from their friends' houses and is at home, waiting for my phone call. I'm guessing you'll be here overnight, so they can stay with me or with Kerry. I can also contact Mom and Dad if you'd—"

"Don't," she interrupted. "They've looked forward to this trip for a long time, and I don't want them to cut it short on my account. They'll be home in a few days anyway. We'll manage."

Zach studied her. "Are you sure?"

"Positive." She sighed. "I wish Zane would call from wherever he is."

"I do, too." Zach shared an emotional bond with his brother that only a twin could claim. If Zane hurt, Zach felt his pain. If Zane was happy, Zach knew it, too. Although the rest of the family couldn't quite understand Zane's tendency toward dangerous pursuits since his wife was killed in a car accident, Zach did. As for

Zane's current status, all Zach could say was that his brother—for the moment—was alive and well. He wouldn't be surprised if one of his rare letters arrived any day now.

The door opened, and Dr. Hall came in. "I just want to check your arm again," she said in her calm voice. Zach jumped off the bed to move out of her way. He watched Leslie study Melinda's fingers, wondering if they appeared more blue than the last time or if the coloration was simply a trick of the lighting. He fixed his gaze on Leslie's face, trying to read the thoughts that lay hidden behind her placid expression.

"Thank you," she said politely before she left the room. A few minutes later, she returned with Dr. Stone in tow. Clearly, something had caused her concern if she'd summoned the cavalry so fast.

Dr. Stone's jovial bedside manner contrasted sharply with Dr. Hall's more serious demeanor. He joked with Melinda as he, too, examined her hand and took her pulse.

"We can't wait any longer," he announced. "It's off to surgery you go."

"What about the problem with the blood?" Zach asked.

"Having units available is purely a precaution and not a necessity," Dr. Stone remarked. "Right now, repairing the damage and restoring the circulation outweigh the risks of not having compatible blood on hand. Not to worry, though," he said as he patted Melinda's shoulder. "You'll be fine. See you upstairs in a few minutes. I'll be the fellow wearing the mask."

He chuckled, Melinda laughed, and Zach watched a grin tug at the corners of Leslie Hall's mouth. He wondered what it would take to draw a full-fledged smile

out of her, and he flashed his lopsided grin at her. For
a few seconds, fate granted his wish and he saw a gentle
smile appear on her face. To his surprise and regret, she
steeled her features behind her now-familiar professional mask before she busied herself flipping through
Melinda's chart.

Dr. Stone left, and a nurse joined them. Leslie turned
to Zach. For some reason, he thought of her more as
Leslie than as Dr. Hall.

"I'm afraid you'll need to leave so we can get her
ready," she said. "Dr. Stone will look for you in the
surgical waiting room upstairs as soon as he's finished."

"How long will it take?"

"I'd plan on several hours before she's in recovery."

Feeling extraneous and properly dismissed, he bent
over and kissed Melinda's cheek. "See you in a little
bit, Mel."

Melinda gripped his hand. "Tell the kids I love
them."

"I will, but you can tell them yourself when you're
awake."

He closed the door behind him with a quiet snick,
then strode into the May sunshine to use the cell phone
he'd left in his truck. Because the hospital prohibited
its use inside the building, he hadn't bothered bringing
it with him. Now he was glad for an excuse to walk
outside and breathe in fresh air.

He called Zane's ranch number and updated Kerry
on Melinda's condition. "There isn't any rush for you
to get here," he told her, "but I'm sure she'd like to
see Nancy and Ryan as soon as she's able. Also, since
my place is on your way, I'd appreciate it if you'd bring
a change of clothes for me." Once Melinda came

through surgery, he intended to make use of his parents'
bathroom facilities, thanks to the set of keys they had
insisted he keep while they were gone.

"Will do."

Next, he spoke to his niece, eight-year-old Nancy,
and his nephew, six-year-old Ryan, reassuring them
about their mother.

After calling his ranch manager to let him know what
was happening, he headed toward the waiting room on
the second floor, where once again he did the only thing
he could.

He paced.

"DR. HALL? Here's the report on Zachary Dumas that
you requested."

"Thanks, Betty." Leslie accepted the form from the
nurse and glanced at the printout. Type A, Rh positive,
appeared in bold letters, which meant that he couldn't
donate blood to his type B, Rh negative sister. It would
have been nice if he had been a match, but lucky breaks
were often in short supply. Still, the odds were good
that Melinda wouldn't require a transfusion or could get
by with plasma, instead.

"I'll be in my office if you need me," she told the
woman.

"Should I page Mr. Dumas for you?"

"That won't be necessary. I know where he is." For
the past several minutes, she'd toyed with thoughts of
joining him upstairs so he wouldn't have to wait alone.
Where those thoughts had come from, she didn't quite
know. She'd never worried about other people under
similar circumstances, but somehow Zach was a different story. Maybe she felt sorry for him because he
seemed so totally out of his element in the hospital en-

vironment. It didn't take any effort to picture him in wide-open spaces, surrounded by bawling cattle on acres of green pastureland under a crisp, blue sky.

She quickly dispelled the image. If she gave in to her impulse, she'd throw away the emotional distance she'd worked so hard to achieve. She couldn't do that. Not yet.

Leslie strode into her office and sank onto her chair. She placed the report on top of her cluttered desk and stared blankly at the words on the page.

Zachary Dumas. Zach.

Reading his name on the sheet of paper conjured up a mental picture of him. The more casual form of his name fit him as well as his faded blue jeans and the blended scents of leather and horse. Some might wrinkle their noses, but she didn't find the combination at all unpleasant.

It had been a long time since she'd met someone who reminded her of the differences between men and women. After her husband's death, she hadn't expected or *wanted* to feel the tug of attraction, but today she had, and she wasn't sure that she enjoyed the feeling. Perhaps it had happened today because she'd been alone for two long years. Or maybe she'd noticed Zach because she'd put in several fourteen-hour days and was too tired to shore up her normal defenses.

Or maybe you saw Zach through different eyes because it's time to move forward, a little voice insisted.

No, she argued. She *had* moved forward. She'd left California and the bad memories to start a new life in the Reno area where she'd been born and where few knew of her recent past. She'd also learned to rely on exhaustion and not pills to lull her to sleep at night, and had returned to the medical profession she loved.

She was making progress.

Unfortunately, Zach's presence would destroy her newly found peace. She'd read the interest in his eyes in spite of her distant manner, and she suspected that Zach Dumas wasn't a man who took no for an answer.

He'd simply have to learn that no was the only answer she could give him, even if one glance from him did funny things to her blood pressure.

She was tempted to let Dr. Stone pass along Zach's test results so she wouldn't have to feel the heat rising between them. After all, once patients and their families left her department, they were no longer her concern. Unfortunately, she couldn't foist this duty on the surgeon. For one thing, she was the ordering physician. For another, she'd promised Zach.

Postponing the inevitable wouldn't make the meeting easier. The sooner she shared Zach's results with him, the sooner she could return to the relative safety of the ER and push him out of her mind.

After checking her pager and telling Betty where she was going, Leslie took the stairs to the second floor and paused outside the surgery waiting room. From her vantage point in the doorway, she saw Zach in the company of another woman and two young children. With one arm around the girl standing next to him and the other balancing a little boy perched on his left knee, he appeared at ease as he laughed at something the boy said. Obviously, he was a doting uncle to Melinda's children, and the woman—his wife?—adored them, as well. A combination of jealousy and longing filled her as she saw evidence of their close-knit family. At the same time, the knowledge that Zach might be attached, and therefore off-limits, was bittersweet.

For some reason, she hated to disrupt the domestic

scene, but she refused to get caught gazing at them like a kid at a candy counter. She squared her shoulders and crossed the threshold.

Immediately, Zach's attention swung in her direction. With one raised brown eyebrow, he released the girl and lifted the boy off his knee before he rose.

"How's Melinda?" he asked.

Leslie walked toward him. "Last I knew, she was doing fine. I thought you'd be interested in knowing the results of your blood tests."

"I am."

The brunette interrupted. "I'll take the kids down to the cafeteria for a snack. They're getting a little antsy."

"Sure thing," Zach said. He turned toward Leslie. "By the way, this is my sister Kerry."

That explained why they appeared so natural together. "Pleased to meet you," Leslie murmured.

Kerry left, the children chattering like magpies, while Leslie stood next to Zach, unsettled at the thought of being alone with him.

The attraction she'd repressed a few minutes ago burst into life again as she noticed the details that made Zach Dumas so appealing. He stood several inches over six feet, and with his muscular build made her feel like a midget at five seven. His brown hair matched the color of the tumbleweeds that blew across the roads and collected in the ditches and along the fences in late summer. Although it was mid May and not yet tanning weather, his face showed signs of exposure to the elements.

All in all, he was an extremely handsome man, and her mind suddenly went blank.

"You have my test results?" he prompted.

"Oh, yes." Leslie pulled her thoughts together and

met his gaze, drawn by the unique sage-green color of his eyes. "You're an A positive. Melinda is B negative, so I'm afraid you can't be a blood donor for her. I'm sorry."

CHAPTER TWO

"WE'RE NOT the same type?" Zach echoed.

"No," Leslie said. "You're not even close."

"Damn." He'd hoped their blood would match.

"Don't be too upset. Having compatible blood on hand is only a precaution."

"I know. I just like to avoid potential problems." As a rancher, he knew how often unforeseen emergencies cropped up in life, and he'd always tried to decrease the odds. Granted, he couldn't change the weather or affect the cattle market, but he'd learned to read Mother Nature's subtle signs and to keep close tabs on commodity trading. He'd suffered his share of losses like everyone else in this business, yet he'd managed to recover. Operating successfully required staying one step ahead, not one step behind.

If his livelihood hadn't taught him that cardinal rule, his marriage had. *Nip problems in the bud,* his father had always said, and if Zach had applied that lesson to his personal life, he might have kept his family intact. Still, Melinda's situation was beyond his control, and he would simply have to trust in the skill and abilities of her doctors.

"Don't we all," Leslie said lightly. "But I'm confident that your sister will handle her surgery just fine."

"You're not just telling me what I want to hear, are you?"

She tilted her head ever so slightly. As the fine strands of her chin-length hair swirled against her face, he wondered if they felt as silky as they looked. "Do you *want* me to tell you what you want to hear?"

He shook his head and grinned sheepishly. "No. Forewarned is forearmed."

Her smile was faint. "I don't say anything that I don't mean. Dr. Stone is one of the best in the city. Your sister couldn't be in finer or more capable hands."

"I appreciate knowing that," he said.

She glanced at her watch. "You shouldn't have to wait much longer before you hear a progress report."

From the tone of her voice, he knew a goodbye would come next. "You're not leaving yet, are you? I know you're busy, but..."

"But what?" she prompted.

He thought fast. He wanted her to stay because he had a feeling that once she walked through that door, he wouldn't see her again. He could come to the ER with a broken leg, but that seemed a little too drastic to suit him.

Something about her seemed familiar, and he wanted to determine exactly why. Normally, he would have asked point-blank, but she'd probably think he was giving her the standard pickup line. As gorgeous as she was, she must field a dozen such pitches a day from every male patient who had reached puberty. It would definitely explain why she treated him so dispassionately.

"I thought we could talk." He winced at what had burst out of his mouth. If his ex-wife had heard him, she would have rolled on the floor laughing. According to her, he didn't know how to hold a conversation unless cattle, horses and ranching concerns were the main subjects.

"What about?"

From the way her shoulders stiffened and her voice took on a decided chill with those two words, she obviously expected him to broach more personal topics. Although he'd love to ask her to dinner, he knew that if he did, she'd shoot down his invitation before he had a chance to finish his sentence. He recognized a skittish animal when he saw one, and the delectable doctor was as nervous as one of his brother's Arabian fillies.

Easy does it, fella, he told himself. "I was hoping we could talk about my test results."

"What do you want to know?"

He heard a relieved note in her voice and mentally patted himself on the back for his quick thinking. "I have a degree in agribusiness and animal husbandry, so I know about DNA sequences and the rules of dominant and recessive inheritance, but I'm a little rusty on those issues," he admitted. "Is it common for brothers and sisters to have different blood types?"

She shrugged. "Of course. It all depends on the parents' genotype and is a matter of probabilities. In your case, either one or both of your parents supplied you with the dominant A gene while your sister received a dominant B."

"So one could be a type A and the other a type B?"

"Or type AB," she said.

Her explanation confirmed what he remembered, but something about this seemed odd. "Then one of our parents can't be a type O?"

Leslie shook her head. "Not a chance."

"My father had his hip replaced several years ago," he said slowly as he tried to sort out everything in his mind. "I remember teasing him that the blood he was getting was as common as an old boot around the bunk-house."

"Type O red cells can be given to everyone, which is why those people are known as universal donors. Although we usually transfuse type-specific red cells, sometimes we can't. There are a number of reasons the blood bank may have cross-matched a substitute."

"If you say so."

"You don't seem convinced."

He shrugged. "I'm sure there's a reasonable explanation. I'd just like to know what it is, or was."

"We may never know the circumstances. The details don't matter as long as the lab issues compatible units."

"You're right." If his father was indeed type O as he suspected, only one scenario could explain Zach's blood type, and it was too shocking to believe.

The family had always teased the boys about certain traits that were different from everyone else's. No one in their household could draw a straight line, much less a picture, and no one could carry a tune. On rare occasions, he wondered if his artistic abilities had been passed down through his mother's or his father's side, but no one seemed to know. Now those simple questions took on new importance.

Part of him wanted to forget the entire incident, but this subject was too crucial to stuff back in its box. He might ignore it for a time, but as surely as he was standing here, it would come back to haunt him at some future date. His father, Hamilton, had taught his children to face their problems, and Zach didn't intend to ignore that lesson now.

"Is there any way we can verify my parents' blood types?"

"Sure. Their family physician can order the tests."

"I meant, without having an actual test."

"We could do a record search." She studied him for a moment. "This is important to you, isn't it?"

He shrugged. "It's more curiosity than anything. For all we know, one of my parents could be a donor for Melinda."

"I'll look into it," she said. "It will take time for someone to sift through the documents, though."

"How long?"

"The staff in the records department could have it in about a week."

"A week?"

She raised an eyebrow. "Your family's charts aren't the only ones we have to handle. Can you guess how many people come through here in a day's time?"

He hurried to make amends. "I understand they're busy. I just thought it would take a few hours."

She chewed on her lower lip in apparent indecision. "I could probably find out in a day or two if I researched it myself," she said with obvious reluctance. "It would be much easier and faster to ask your parents. I'm sure they can tell you their blood types immediately."

"Probably," he agreed. "But they're out of town, and I'd rather not call them. I'd have to explain about Melinda, and once they know she's had an accident, they'll drive day and night to get here."

"And you don't want them to worry," she said softly.

Leslie's gentle smile did strange things to his insides. He was proud to think that he had coaxed it out of her and was selfish enough to want to see it all the time. "Yeah."

"All right, I'll do what I can. Is tomorrow soon enough for you?"

He flashed her his most beguiling smile. "Tomorrow is great. I owe you one."

"Uncle Zach, Uncle Zach." The excited voices of his niece and nephew interrupted his plan to set a time and place when they could meet again. He hid his disappointment as he caught the two children barreling toward him, each sporting an orange mustache.

"What's up, guys?" he asked.

"Aunt Kerry bought us orange pop," Ryan told him as he licked his upper lip. "I never had orange pop before. I think it's my favorite."

Nancy rolled her eyes in an eight-year-old's imitation of a teenager. "Every flavor you drink is your favorite. Yesterday it was grape, and last week it was—"

He glowered at his sister. "I can change my mind if I want. Can't I, Uncle Zach?"

"You sure can, cowboy," Zach answered, ruffling the boy's hair. He glanced at Leslie, expecting to see her smile, but he was surprised to see her professional persona firmly in place.

She rose. "Dr. Stone shouldn't be much longer. I'll get back to you as soon as I can."

"Thanks." Patting his chest pockets for the small pad and pencil he always carried, he said, "I'll give you my number."

"Are you in the phone book?"

"Yes."

"Then I'll find it." Before he could offer to save her the trouble, she hurried from the room, her white coat flapping against her long legs. He hated to see her leave, but she had responsibilities elsewhere, responsibilities that took precedence over visiting with a patient's family member.

Kerry waved her hand in his face. "This is a surprise," she said with a twinkle in her blue eyes and a teasing lilt in her voice. "I never would have believed it if I hadn't seen it for myself."

"What are you talking about?"

"Zach Dumas trying to give his number to a woman. I thought it usually worked the opposite way."

A sheepish grin curved his lips. "Dare to be different."

"I'll keep it in mind," she said dryly. "Although I'm dying of curiosity. You've been out of circulation for a while, so where did you learn your new strategy?"

"It's not what you think."

"And what do I think?"

Zach inclined his head in the direction of Nancy and Ryan, who at the moment were bickering over who should have control of the television remote. "Little ears."

Kerry lowered her voice to a whisper. "And what *should* I think?"

"She's looking up some medical information for me. When she finds it, she'll call me. End of story." He hoped it wouldn't be the end, but his cousin-slash-adopted-sister didn't have to know all the nitty-gritty details.

"Uh-huh." She didn't sound convinced. "What sort of *medical* information is she researching for you?"

He revised the facts slightly. "She's going to see if Mom or Dad could be a possible blood donor for Melinda."

The blue hue of her eyes darkened as she narrowed her gaze. "I thought she only broke her arm."

''She did.'' He dutifully repeated both Leslie's and Dr. Stone's official line. ''Having blood on hand is a precautionary measure. Apparently she has a rare antibody or something, and the doctors were trying to be prepared in case of a problem.''

He purposely didn't mention the questions Leslie had raised when she'd relayed his lab results. The family had enough on their plate without worrying about something that probably wasn't a problem in the first place. When this was all over, he'd laugh at himself for thinking such crazy thoughts and forget all about it.

Kerry smiled. ''And if she doesn't call you, you have the perfect excuse to contact her.''

He grinned. ''Exactly.''

''Well, Zach. I'm absolutely impressed. I thought the closest I'd ever see you to a woman again was when one of the waitresses at Armando's took your dinner order. You've restored my faith in you.''

''Thanks. I think.''

''Although I figured you'd go for someone who's a little more…'' Her sentence trailed off as if she couldn't think of a way to finish it.

''Outgoing?'' he supplied.

''Relaxed.''

''Leslie is a doctor,'' he reminded her. ''I'm sure she wants her patients and colleagues to take her seriously.''

''That's probably it.''

He couldn't contain the question hovering at the back of his mind. ''Does she look familiar to you?''

Kerry shook her head. ''No. Why?''

He shrugged. ''I'm sure I've seen her before, but I just can't place her.''

''Maybe it was in the ER after one of your Saturday night brawls,'' she said wryly.

"I'm caught in the middle of one drunken fight and you never forget it," he protested. "And if you recall, I was only a bystander. I came to the ER because Luke wasn't in any shape to drive himself."

She grinned. "A likely story."

"Believe me, if Leslie had been on duty, it wouldn't have mattered how many face punches I took. I wouldn't have forgotten her."

THE MAN *is unforgettable.* Leslie idly murmured polite greetings and nodded briefly to her colleagues on her way to the emergency room as she replayed those few moments in the surgical waiting room. Ever since she'd met him, he'd stuck to her thoughts like a tenacious sandbur. Why, she didn't know. He was the total opposite of every male she'd ever dated, including the man she'd eventually married.

Her college classes in chemistry, biology, physics and calculus had been filled with aspiring students like her. Not one of them, nor any since, resembled the tall, lanky cowboy who possessed rock-hard biceps, callused hands and eyes that saw more than most. He smelled of fresh air, honest sweat and leather, instead of a fragrance out of a bottle. His scent was a far cry from the sterile, antiseptic aroma that surrounded her day in and day out.

Perhaps it was the sound of his voice that had made its mark on her, she mused. The deep baritone was soothing, and she could easily imagine the tone causing the most fractious animal to settle down and do whatever Zach asked.

Yet the more she thought about the situation, the more she rationalized her disturbing inability to forget him. He *was* different from other men, and that was why she couldn't wipe him out of her mind easily. The fact that she was slightly envious didn't help matters, either.

Actually, she was more than slightly envious. On a scale of one to ten, she was a twelve. During those few moments when she'd seen him with Melinda, and then with his other sister, Kerry, the bond between them was unmistakable. She'd wanted a sibling more than anything, but as an only child of divorced parents, it wasn't in the cards. How lucky they were to have each other to lean on during tough times, and from the way they stuck together, they obviously realized it, too.

As she walked through the ER fingering the sturdy chain at her neck, she was forced to admit that this was her world, and Zach Dumas didn't have any part in it. She should have simply told him to discuss his concerns about his parents' blood type with their family physician, but the plea in his green eyes had made her comment die unspoken. Somehow, he'd made her feel as if she were the only one who could help him.

Now, away from his boyish charm and masculine magnetism, she could think straight. She'd locate the information for him, place a simple phone call and then push him out of her life.

It was for the best.

Betty, the twenty-five-year-old redheaded ER nurse who possessed an uncanny ability to turn her shapeless scrubs into a fashion statement, joined her at the desk. "You look rather grim. Bad news?"

Leslie cleared away the frown on her face. "No. Why do you ask?" Although almost everyone accepted that Leslie wasn't inclined to discuss her personal life with staff, Betty wasn't as obliging. The nurse liked to talk about everything under the sun, and sometimes Leslie bent her rule, but for the most part, she placed definite restrictions on their friendship. She harbored too many secrets and had too much at stake to relax her guard. One wrong word, and she would be forced to start over. Again.

"You didn't seem too happy for a minute there. I thought Melinda Dumas might have run into complications."

"As far as I know, everything is fine." Leslie pulled out a chair and sat down at the nurses' station.

"How's her brother?"

"He's fine, too." For pity's sake. She was starting to sound like a recording, and not a very good one, at that.

Betty nodded thoughtfully. "I'd have to agree with you. Zach Dumas is one mighty fine guy. Most women would be turning handsprings to spend a few minutes alone with him."

Leslie tried to sound noncommittal. "He seems nice enough."

"Nice enough? My goodness, every female I know would do anything to catch his eye." She leaned closer. "So how does it feel?"

"How does what feel?"

"Knowing that Zach Dumas, one of the wealthiest ranchers in the state, has noticed you?"

Leslie felt her face warm as if she'd received an instant sunburn. "He has not," she protested.

"I saw him when you were drawing his blood. Most men aren't thrilled when a woman comes at 'em with a needle, but I'd bet he didn't feel a thing."

"Of course he didn't. I'm good with sharp instruments."

Betty shook her head. "That may be, but I'll bet if you check your coat sleeve, you'll find drool marks."

"Oh, for heaven's sake," Leslie said as she rolled her eyes. "We have absolutely nothing in common."

"How do you know? You weren't together long enough to find out."

"The length of time doesn't matter. After those few minutes, I can give you a list." Leslie ticked off the points on her fingers. "As a rancher, he's an outdoors sort of fellow. He goes to one of the cowboy hangouts on Saturday nights, chugs beer and plays pool with his buddies. His favorite food is beef. Although he prefers a thick, juicy steak, he'll eat anything smothered in barbecue sauce."

Betty giggled. "You're stereotyping."

"Maybe, but you know I'm right."

"Variety is the spice of life."

"Working here provides all the spice I could possibly need, so don't start spreading any rumors," Leslie warned. "I won't be seeing him again."

"Leslie, Leslie, Leslie," Betty singsonged. "You're missing a marvelous opportunity."

"If I am, it won't be the first," she said calmly. "Think of it this way. Some other woman now has a chance at him." As far as Leslie could tell, her biggest mistake was to get involved in Zach's family's concerns. The sooner she took care of her obligation, the sooner she could return to her peaceful, safe, albeit boring existence.

"By the way," Leslie continued, "do you know of an easy way to find out someone's blood type, other than going through his or her medical records?"

"Sure. Call the blood bank. My cousin works in the lab and she says they keep a card file on everyone who has their blood typed or cross-matched."

"Great." Leslie punched in the four-digit phone extension and identified herself to the woman who answered before making her request. "I'm following up on Melinda Dumas's case. Do you have any records for Eleanor or Hamilton Dumas? They're her parents."

"I'll check." A minute later, the woman returned. "Do you have any birth dates or social security numbers to cross-reference?"

"Sorry."

"Without a date of birth, I can't be certain that these are the same people you're looking for. According to our files, though, Eleanor Dumas is B negative and Hamilton Dumas is O positive."

Leslie paused as she wrote both results on a notepad in front of her and followed them with question marks. "Are you sure?"

"Positive," the technologist said cheerfully. "Mr. Dumas received four units of his blood type in nineteen ninety-eight."

"Thanks." She replaced the receiver. The situation, which had seemed so straightforward a short time ago, was now shrouded in mystery and complications. Telling Zach what she'd discovered wouldn't be easy.

Hamilton Dumas could not be his biological father.

CHAPTER THREE

"HEY, SIS. Are you ready to fly this coop?" Zach strode into Melinda's hospital room two days later to find Melinda seated on the edge of her bed, wearing the fresh clothes he'd brought yesterday.

"What a question," she said with a tired smile. "I was ready to leave an hour ago, but the doctor hasn't come by to sign my discharge papers yet. They charge by the minute, you know. I shudder to think what those two painkillers I took this morning will cost me."

"Not to worry," he teased, trying to take her mind off her money troubles. "You can hire out Nancy and Ryan. I'm always looking for good slave labor."

"Like you'd get any work done at all with those two underfoot," she grumbled. Her tone had become good-natured, so Zach was pleased he'd been able to lighten her mood.

"Speaking of those two, where are they?" she asked.

"At Zane's, waiting for you. They've planned a welcome home celebration, so act surprised."

"You didn't leave them alone in the kitchen, did you?" she asked, clearly horrified. "The last time Nancy tried to make brownies—"

"Don't worry. Kerry won't let them burn down the house."

"Thank goodness."

Zach noticed the cart loaded with her overnight bag

and the assorted flower arrangements she'd received. "Do you have everything?"

"Everything except the nurse with the wheelchair," she said. "I wonder where she is. I don't mind telling you that I can't leave soon enough."

"What's the rush? You won't have peace and quiet at home."

"Ha! You haven't stayed in the hospital for a while. I've had more peace and quiet when we were snowed in at the ranch for a week with two kids who had cabin fever."

"It can't be that bad."

"Humph." Melinda glared at him. "Besides, I've felt guilty for taking you away from your work. You're so busy this time of year."

He shrugged off her objections. "Spring is always busy, but then, so are the other seasons. To be honest, I don't mind taking an afternoon off to keep you company."

She smiled. "Of course, I'm not sure if it's me you've been coming to see or the lady doctor."

He grinned. "Why, you're the light of my life, sis."

"Get serious. You won't hurt my feelings if you admit you're interested in Dr. Hall."

"I wouldn't object to spending a few hours with her," he confessed. "The opportunity just hasn't arisen. It will, though."

"As much as I'd like to help you with your love life, I'm not staying another day," she warned.

"I don't need your help."

Melinda's eyes narrowed. "You sound awfully certain. You're not planning to do something that will send you to the ER, are you?"

"Isn't there a syndrome where women doctors fall in love with their patients?" he asked innocently.

"Oh, for pete's sake. I think you've fallen off your horse and landed one too many times on your head."

"Gee, sis. I'm not that desperate. Or stupid. Leslie was supposed to call me yesterday about Mom and Dad's blood type, but she must have been busy because she didn't. I stopped by the ER before I came up here, but she was with a patient, so I'll catch her on the way out."

"Ah, I get it. And then you'll invite her to dinner as your payment for her taking time to hunt down the information."

He grinned. "You're as sharp as a tack, sis."

The slightly ajar door opened, and Melinda's nurse, a short, friendly young woman, pushed in a wheelchair and parked it near the bed. "Dr. Stone just called. He'll be here within the next thirty minutes to discharge you."

"Good," Melinda said.

The nurse left on soundless feet, and Zach made an instant decision. "Since we have to wait, if you don't mind, I'll track down Leslie."

Melinda clicked on the television. "Go ahead, but don't forget that you only have half an hour."

Zach didn't need further encouragement. He arrived at the emergency room in record time and was delighted to see Leslie seated behind the nurses' station desk. "Hi," he said. "I stopped by earlier, but you were busy."

Leslie rose, looking as fresh as the flowers at a florist's shop. "So I hear."

"I was afraid you'd tried to call yesterday and hadn't been able to reach me." He offered it as an excuse although he knew it wasn't valid. He'd stayed close to his cell phone all day.

When she met his gaze, something in her eyes didn't seem quite right. "Things came up, and I couldn't contact you. Look," she began, "this really isn't a good time for us to talk."

He glanced around the department. Earlier, the place had been filled with people, but now the halls were quiet. However, he wasn't about to argue, especially since it made his next offer all the more logical. "Fine," he said. "I'll meet you later and we can discuss this over dinner."

"Tonight?" She shook her head. "I can't."

"How about tomorrow?"

"Um..." She glanced away before meeting his gaze. "All right. I suppose I can spare a few minutes now."

He followed her to an empty exam cubicle, puzzled by her actions. Did he make her that nervous? If so, he was surprised she didn't offer to send his results in the mail. "What did you find out?"

Leslie closed the door behind them. "Your mother is B negative. Maybe when she returns, your family physician could order further studies to see if she could be a donor for Melinda, should a future need arise."

"That's good news."

"Yes, it is."

Her unwavering gaze alerted his instincts. "And my father?"

She drew a deep breath. "According to our records, Hamilton Dumas received type-specific blood several years ago."

"Which makes him type O."

She nodded. "Yes."

"But then that means..." Zach sank onto the bed,

hardly able to take it all in. Yet a part of him wasn't surprised. The possibility had been percolating at the back of his mind ever since he'd found out his own blood type. He'd simply hoped that he'd jumped to the wrong conclusion.

"Then he can't be my father."

"He can't be your *birth* father," she corrected gently. "If you're talking about the person who comforted you, taught you and raised you to be the man you are today, then Hamilton still *is* your father."

Zach's mind raced with the implications. "So you're saying that my mother had an affair." The concept was inconceivable. His entire family had been devastated to learn of his wife's extramarital relationship with their accountant, and his mother had taken the news harder than most. Was that why? Because she'd been afraid her sins had come home to roost?

"I'm not telling you anything. I'm only relating the facts. And there is another possibility to consider."

"What?"

"You could be adopted."

"Adopted?" This idea was only marginally better than the last one. "Zane and I are thirty-eight years old. Why wouldn't my parents have told us?"

"Who knows? They obviously had their reasons."

"But didn't they think we'd find out?"

"Again, I can't answer that."

"What am I going to tell them? I can't act as if nothing has changed. If I could, I'd be in Hollywood and not busting my butt on a ranch near Reno."

"I understand. More than you know." The misery on her face spoke of her sincerity.

Suddenly, he knew why she hadn't called him yesterday and didn't appear pleased to see him today. "You weren't going to call me, were you?"

"I'd hoped you would forget," she said simply. "People always say that knowledge is power, but there are times when it only creates more problems."

"In other words, ignorance is bliss?"

"In some situations, yes. I knew that once you learned this, your relationship with your family would change, and I'd feel responsible."

"Why should you?"

"Because I'm the one who discovered the discrepancy in the first place."

"Maybe your results are wrong."

"I doubt it. Unless, of course, the birth dates aren't the same." She pulled a piece of paper out of her lab coat pocket and handed it to him. The dates recorded matched the ones he'd known for years.

Zach handed the slip back to her. "They're correct."

She sat beside him and placed a hand on his arm. "What are you going to do?"

He glanced at her, noticing a worried furrow on her forehead. "I don't know. I want to confront them, but if I do, everything will change. If I don't, I'll still have my doubts."

"Which is why I didn't want to tell you."

If there was ever a time when he wanted to talk to Zane, it was now. Unfortunately, Zane had troubles of his own, and unable to face them, he'd gone to South America. As his twin, Zach had felt Zane's pain over the death of his wife, just as Zane had felt Zach's when his marriage had ended. Although he disagreed with his brother's methods, Zach understood his need to get away, to take risks and to find a new purpose in his life. It was damn inconvenient, though, for Zane to leave the country and disappear in some jungle where he couldn't be reached. Zach could only rely on his mental radar and hope it would be strong enough to bridge the distance.

"Take your time deciding what it is you want to do," she continued softly. "A few more days, or weeks, won't matter."

"I suppose not."

Her pager bleeped, and she squeezed his arm before she rose. "I have to go."

"I do, too. I told Melinda I wouldn't take more than thirty minutes."

Leslie paused at the door. "For what it's worth, Zach, I'm sorry."

He nodded. "I know. Thanks."

As he headed upstairs, he felt numb. He couldn't imagine his mother having an affair, and not just because she was his mother. It was impossible to envision her with another man because she'd always been so devoted to his father. Her *husband*, he corrected. The only logical explanation was adoption, as Leslie had suggested, but that, too, seemed far-fetched. Yet he and his brother had to come from somewhere.

Outside Melinda's door, he paused and forced a smile. Until he sorted things out and decided upon his next move, no one would know what he'd learned. As Leslie had said, there were times when ignorance was bliss.

"Are you ready to go, sis?" he asked. His nickname for her slipped out an instant before he realized what he'd said. If Eleanor and Hamilton weren't his parents, then Melinda wasn't his sister, and Nancy and Ryan weren't his niece and nephew. The only ones he could claim as his own were his brother and his ten-year-old sons, Keith and Kenny.

Leslie hadn't just knocked his parents off their pedestal. She'd pulled the ground out from under him. Everything he'd ever believed in, counted on, had just collapsed like a house of cards. It would take time for him to rebuild his identity, which was a sad state of affairs for a man who was pushing forty.

"I was getting ready to page you," Melinda said. "Did everything go okay with Dr. Hall?"

"Yeah, sure. Why wouldn't it?" He forced himself to look directly at her. Otherwise, she'd know he wasn't being totally honest.

"Just wondering. So, big brother," she teased, "are you taking her to dinner?"

"She's busy right now, and as you said, this time of year is crazy for me, too."

"Oh, Zach. She said no, didn't she?"

Come to think of it, she hadn't answered him at all. "We left things open-ended."

"At least she didn't tell you to take a hike."

"No, she didn't." *That* would have been a rejection he could have handled. "So," he said as he glanced around the room one last time, "are you ready?"

If Melinda noticed his sudden hurry to leave, she didn't comment. Then again, her desire to put distance between herself and the West View Hospital exceeded his own. While she wanted to see her children and relax in familiar surroundings, he wanted to hop on Jim Dandy, his Appaloosa, and head for his favorite thinking spot. Hearing the water trickle over the rock bed and feeling the wind rustle through his hair made it easier for a man to regain his perspective when he had a burden that he couldn't share with anyone.

Where in the hell are you, Zane?

"Is something on your mind, Zach?" Eleanor asked a week later as she poured both her husband and Zach a cup of coffee.

Instantly, he went on alert. He thought he'd done a remarkable job of hiding his inner turmoil since his parents had returned home three days ago. "Why do you ask?"

Hamilton chuckled. At seventy-two, he bore all the signs of years of ranching. His face was weathered by the elements, his skin as tough as leather, and he refused to wear anything but jeans and a plaid cotton shirt. For special occasions, he added a bolo tie and the fanciest silver belt buckle he owned.

"You never could fool your mother, son. What makes you think you can now? I guessed you had somethin' weighin' on you since we've only seen you once in the last week."

"I've been busy," Zach defended. "You know how hectic spring is."

Eleanor sat across from him at the table. She'd recently passed her seventieth birthday, and Zach remembered how she'd prided herself on being able to wear her wedding gown for their fiftieth anniversary. As he studied her, he saw the inner strength that allowed her to retain her sense of humor in spite of all the troubles she'd faced during her lifetime. Raising twin sons who'd been far from angelic, going without when the ranch's financial picture looked bleak and dealing with his father's ill health in recent years hadn't been easy. Although her face had its share of lines, laughter had deepened most of them.

"I can always tell the difference between my children being busy and when they're struggling with a problem. You get quiet, and a certain wrinkle shows up on your forehead. Zane gets adventuresome and disappears."

"You know us pretty well," he said with a smile.

"After all these years, I should. It's a shame that Monica didn't take time to learn, too. I still don't understand how she could possibly have turned to *that man*."

Since learning of Monica's affair with Tom Patterson, their former accountant, his mother always referred to Tom as *that man*. Zach preferred to use stronger language whenever he thought of the man who'd betrayed him.

"Well, she did," he said, aware that the pain of his wife's leaving had subsided long ago. While he didn't miss Monica, he missed his sons all the time. Their twice monthly weekend visits weren't nearly long enough, and he hoped to convince his ex-wife to change the custody arrangements now that the boys were getting older. There were some things in life that were better taught by a father, and how to become a responsible man was one of them.

"It's in the past, and we have to forget it and move on." As he spoke those words, he wondered if his subconscious was sending him a message about his current dilemma. After spending any spare minute he could find this past week at the river winding through the Twin Bar Ranch, he knew he couldn't move forward until he discovered what had happened thirty-eight years ago.

"You're right, dear." Eleanor patted his hand. "We must. But something is on your mind. I have a feeling it concerns Melinda. Is there something she's not telling us?"

Part of his dilemma had been how to broach the subject. Now his mother had given him the perfect lead, and he grabbed it.

"Melinda is fine," he said. "The doctors had a question about her blood type, though."

"After she had two babies there, what sort of question could they have about her blood?" Hamilton's voice rose an octave.

"Relax, Dad," he soothed. "It's just that the hospital couldn't find any units that were compatible, so because I'm a family member—" he flinched at his explanation "—they tested me."

"And?" Eleanor demanded.

"Mine didn't match, either. I'm an A positive and Mel is a B negative." Anticipating her next question, he continued. "Luckily, Mel didn't need a transfusion, after all. But we—Dr. Hall, actually—checked the records. You're a B negative and Dad is an O positive."

"Then I could be a match for her," Eleanor said.

"Yes."

"Well, that's not such a problem."

He winced. Mentioning the next part was like opening Pandora's box. Once he did, he'd never be able to close the lid. Yet his need to know overruled his reservations.

"That's not all." At her raised eyebrow, he continued. "You and…Dad—" again he stumbled over the name as he glanced at his father "—can't have a child who's A positive. It's genetically impossible."

The look on his parents' faces would have been comical if the situation wasn't so serious. "What are you asking us, son?" Eleanor queried.

He drew a deep breath as he rubbed the back of his neck. "There are only two possibilities for why my blood type doesn't match yours."

"Are you implying that I had an affair before you were born?" the mother's voice was slightly incredulous.

Hamilton visibly bristled and rose halfway out of his chair. Although he appeared much less robust than he had been ten years ago, he was still stronger than most men his age. "You apologize to your mother, boy. I don't care how old you are. You don't have any right to make such an accusation."

Eleanor quickly placed a hand on her husband's arm. "Now, Hamilton. Let's hear what Zach has to say."

With a sniff, Hamilton sat down.

"I'm not accusing anyone of anything," Zach said. "I'm only telling you what the facts indicate."

Hamilton's face took on a ruddy hue. "Your mother didn't have an affair, so put that thought right out of your mind."

Zach glanced at his mother as she stood behind Hamilton's chair. She placed her hands on his shoulders in a familiar gesture of love and support. Instead of mirroring Hamilton's anger, her eyes twinkled with merriment.

"No, dear. I never had an affair. Believe me. I didn't have the energy or the stamina to juggle *two* men in my life. Hamilton was more than enough."

Her clear-eyed gaze was enough to dispel Zach's doubts on that score. Both his parents had taught him and his siblings to tell the truth, no matter the cost, and he couldn't imagine them going against their own teachings.

"I believe you," he said calmly.

Hamilton patted his wife's veined hand before Zach felt his glare. "You should."

"The only other explanation for the results would be if Zane and I were adopted."

This time, his mother burst out laughing. "Well, dear, after suffering through nearly twenty-four hours of hard labor, I can assure you that you were not adopted."

"Good God, son." Hamilton sounded exasperated. "Where in the Sam Hill are you getting these ideas?"

He wanted to believe his parents, but he couldn't argue with the facts. "The evidence indicates—"

"Now, son. You and Zane are our boys just as sure as the good Lord made little green apples. You're tall, dark-haired and as feisty as I was. You both took to riding a horse like you were born to it, because you were."

"How do you explain my artistic ability? No one else in the family can even draw stick people."

Hamilton shrugged. "Somebody along the line probably had talent but never developed it like you did. Children aren't carbon copies of their parents, you know."

Eleanor suddenly snapped her fingers. "I just remembered something to prove that you're not adopted. I'll be right back."

She returned a few moments later carrying a photo album. She placed it on the table, flipped to the middle and pointed to a particular photograph. "See? There we are, the day after you and Zane were born."

Zach had seen the picture before, but this time, he studied it more closely. In it, Eleanor sat in a hospital bed, appearing tired and worn out, but a huge smile covered her face as she cuddled a little bundle in each arm. Hamilton stood beside her, beaming as if he'd invented fatherhood single-handedly.

"There you go," Eleanor said triumphantly. "Believe me, if we'd adopted you two, I would have looked a lot better than I did.''

Zach let out a deep sigh. ''I'm convinced.''

''As you should be,'' Hamilton said. ''It's just not worth tying yourself in knots over crazy notions.''

''But that doesn't explain why my blood type doesn't match the rest of the family's.''

''I can tell you why,'' Hamilton said, leaning back in his chair as he folded his arms across his chest. ''It's as plain as the bumps on a pickle. The hospital made a mistake with your test. It wouldn't be the first time someone in the medical profession made an error. This time, you happened to be the unlucky fellow.''

''It's a rather far-fetched idea, don't you think, Dad?''

''Far-fetched? Tell that to the guy I read about in last night's paper. He went in to have his left foot amputated and lost his right foot, instead. Then there's the fellow who supposedly needed a triple bypass, and after the cardiologist cut him open, he discovered the guy's heart was fine. Someone had mixed up the records. I'll bet the same thing happened to you.''

His father's explanation was the most logical he'd heard so far. Then again, perhaps it was the one he wanted to hear. ''You're probably right.''

''I know I am. So you can go back and tell Dr. Hall that her lab made a mistake.''

Zach slowly smiled. He'd wanted an excuse to see Leslie again, and now he had one. This time, however, when he asked her to dinner, he wouldn't accept any response but yes.

''May I borrow this picture, Mom?'' he asked.

''Of course. Just don't lose it,'' she warned as she

removed the snapshot from its corner mounts. "It's the only copy I have."

"I won't." He accepted the photo and studied it once again. Leslie might not want to admit that the staff at the hospital were fallible, but this was proof that even she couldn't dispute. A picture was worth a thousand words.

CHAPTER FOUR

LESLIE GLANCED with relief at the ER's huge dry-erase board that served as the scheduling center for the department. Names had filled every slot since early that morning, and now all but two had been erased. Those people would be leaving as soon as the lab reports arrived. Then she'd go off duty and leave her department in the capable hands of another physician.

Betty joined her at the nurses' station and shook her head. "That's a bad sign."

"What is?"

She pointed to the board. "The lull before the Friday night storm. It happens every time."

Leslie laughed. "You're superstitious."

"Observant," Betty corrected. "In case you've forgotten, tonight is a full moon. I can guarantee this place will be hopping just as soon as the sun goes down, if not before."

"You're probably right." The full-moon theory was more fact than fantasy. Every ER staffer had firsthand experience with the phenomenon. More births occurred during this time, as well, although those patients usually bypassed her department and went directly to the maternity wing.

"I feel sorry for the fellows working this weekend," Betty said. "Especially since I worked last weekend and it was so quiet it was boring."

"The luck of the draw," Leslie commented.

"Don't I know it. So what are you going to do this evening?" Betty asked as she plopped in a chair and began sifting through a pile of forms.

"Laundry. Run to the grocery store."

"On Friday?" Betty sounded as horrified as she appeared. As far as Leslie knew, she rarely spent any night of the week alone. While Leslie wasn't questioning her morals, she wondered how the woman managed to juggle her schedule so expertly and still have energy to spare.

"Sure, why not?"

"Don't you know it's a crime to stay home and do chores on the start of a weekend?"

Leslie smiled. "I guess my mother neglected to tell me that."

"I know this really nice guy," Betty began.

"No blind dates." On this subject, Leslie was adamant. Actually, her rule included all dates, but she didn't feel the need to enlighten her co-worker, who clearly didn't approve of Leslie's choice of free-time activities. Going into that much detail would require more explanations than Leslie wanted to give. They all knew she was a widow, and as far as she was concerned, that was enough.

"He's really sweet. You two would get along great."

"I'm sure," Leslie said dryly. "Thanks, but no thanks."

"How about joining us for a drink after work? Some of us want to celebrate surviving another week in the trenches."

Leslie was tempted. It seemed like a lifetime since she'd first met Michael after work for a drink and a movie with their friends. Weeks later, they'd made plans for just the two of them, and still later, after they were married, Friday nights had become *their* nights.

Those had been special times, and now that Michael was gone, Fridays had become another day to live through. To keep her mind off what had once been the high point of her week, she filled Friday nights with mind-numbing chores or spent the hours immersed in movie marathons. While she might be overdue in establishing a new routine and making new friends, she wasn't ready to get chummy with her co-workers and colleagues. She wanted someone different, someone who didn't have any ties to the hospital. Someone like...

Zach Dumas.

"I'll think about it," she said.

"Think hard," Betty advised. "After handling that gunshot wound this morning, you deserve to kick up your heels and pat yourself on the back."

While Leslie was proud that she'd kept the man alive long enough to get him to surgery, she also knew that he wasn't out of the woods yet. "I can't take all the credit," she said. "It was a group effort."

"Yeah, well, I don't mind telling you that I thought he was a goner." Betty shook her head. "Men and their guns. All it takes is a hothead, a little alcohol, and somebody gets hurt."

Leslie agreed. As far as she was concerned, firearms should be outlawed, but her views weren't popular in an area where hunting controlled the natural predator population.

"Anyway, we'll meet at Hugo's when happy hour starts," Betty told her. "They serve a great burger if you decide popcorn and pretzels aren't enough. Do you know where it is?"

Leslie passed the club every night on her way home. "Yes."

"Great." Betty left to check the printer for the reports they hadn't received.

With the nurse occupied, Leslie's thoughts drifted to Zach. A week had gone by since she'd delivered her earth-shattering news, and every day she'd wondered how he was doing. It was ridiculous, really. She hadn't let herself get close enough to anyone to worry about their mental well-being in years, but with Zach, she had. Probably because she felt guilty for her role in his dilemma.

By three-thirty, Leslie had sent her last two patients home and was sitting at the nurses' station finishing paperwork. The day shift staff walked by on their way to the exit, those who were off duty this weekend gloating at those who weren't.

Leslie didn't care about being excluded from their conversation. As long as she kept to herself, she didn't feel obligated to share bits and pieces of her life as they all did. Chances were, if they *did* know of the skeletons in both her professional and personal closets, they'd give her a very wide berth. Some people carried distinct prejudices about those who required the services of a mental health professional, so she'd prefer being thought of as standoffish rather than crazy. Yet her intent to remain distant didn't stop her from listening shamelessly to their conversations.

Betty stopped. "Staying late again?"

Leslie smiled. "The job isn't done until the paperwork says it is. I have a few things to finish before I can call it a day."

Betty nodded knowingly. "Like stopping at the ICU?"

Leslie was startled by the nurse's perception. "How did you guess?"

Betty shrugged. "It's simple, really. Whenever we have a bad case that goes upstairs, you stay late. A friend of mine is a nurse in the unit, and she's mentioned how you like to drop in for an update. Since Mr. Laramie gave us a few tense moments, I figured you'd do the same for him."

"I didn't think anyone noticed," Leslie said, wondering if everyone tracked her movements. So much for staying in the background so no one would pay attention to her. Obviously, her actions had fueled staff members' curiosity.

"Most probably don't. I only heard about it because I know Holly. I think it's rather nice of you to take the time. Anyway," Betty continued, apparently losing interest in the subject, "don't forget to join us. We'll hang around at least until seven."

"All right, but if I don't see you, have a great weekend."

"With three days off, how could I possibly not?" Betty left, and ten minutes later, Leslie arrived at the intensive care unit. She recognized the nurse on duty from her previous excursions.

"How is Mr. Laramie, our gunshot victim?" she asked, realizing as she read her name tag that this was Betty's friend Holly.

"Critical, but stable," the brunette answered. "Here's his chart if you want to see for yourself."

"Thanks." Leslie flipped through the nurse's notes, the surgeons' comments and the host of lab reports. The shotgun blast had caused extensive chest and abdominal damage that took hours to repair. If the fragments had blown an inch higher and an inch more to the left, he'd be resting in the morgue and not a hospital bed.

Betty had thought it a nice gesture that Leslie watched her patients' progress after they left the ER. Little did the nurse know her actions had nothing to do with being nice. Leslie kept tabs on these cases because the knowledge that she'd saved another person, another family from the devastation of death brought her tremendous comfort.

She closed the record and handed it to Holly. "He looks good, considering we almost lost him."

"Yeah." Holly slid the chart in bed three's slot. "I hope he'll find less volatile drinking buddies after he leaves us."

Leslie agreed. As she left the unit, she ran into Norman Rice, the chief of West View's emergency services, as he rounded the corner. Norm was a tall man in his early fifties and reminded her of Ichabod Crane. Although he was gruff more often than not, underneath the tough facade was a physician who cared deeply about the welfare of his patients.

"Hi, Leslie," he said. "I'm not used to seeing you outside your territory."

"I just came to check on a fellow who came into the ER this morning."

"Ah, yes. The gunshot victim."

Word obviously traveled fast. "That's him."

"Carter said you did a great job in stabilizing him."

"We have a great staff," she said, unwilling to take sole credit although privately she basked under his compliment. His job included monitoring the quality of the ER department in general and her services in particular, but Leslie waited for the day when he wouldn't look over her shoulder quite so frequently. To his credit, he did so in an unobtrusive manner, and she doubted anyone else was aware of it.

"It was probably tough on you when he came in."

She knew what he was asking. If there were certain situations she couldn't handle, she'd lose her job faster than she could say *emergency*. "All trauma cases are hard," she said, meeting his gaze. "Luckily, this one looks as if it will end well."

Norm patted her on the back. "Aptly put, but this guy definitely owes a big thanks to you. And now, I hate to run, but I'm already late for the wife's dinner party. If I don't get home soon, she'll never forgive me." He grinned.

Leslie smiled. "Have a nice evening."

It was almost six by the time she returned to the ER. Because she intended to stop at the grocery store on her way home, she took a shower in the nurses' lounge and changed into her street clothes. Blow drying her short curls took an extra few minutes before she declared herself presentable. Once in a while, she missed the versatility of shoulder-length hair, but she'd moved to Reno to start over, and a drastically different hairstyle had been part of the change.

Leslie grabbed her purse and her lunch bag from her locker and headed for the exit. As she passed the nurses' station, Gina, the evening shift ward clerk, stopped her.

"Dr. Hall?" she asked. "There's a guy here to see you."

"I'm on my way home. Can't Dr. Parkes deal with him?"

Gina's smile was broad. "He's here to see you, and if you want my opinion, he'll be worth a few minutes of your time."

An image of Zach Dumas shot into her head, but she

disregarded it. Melinda had been discharged, so it couldn't be Zach. It was too late in the day for a salesman, and she'd already seen Dr. Rice. That meant he was either a patient or a relative of Ralph Laramie.

"Did he mention his name?"

"No, but he's waiting by the water fountain. He's been here for nearly half an hour."

Her visitor had probably arrived just minutes after she'd returned from ICU. Leslie glanced in the direction Gina indicated and saw a familiar form leaning against the wall, arms crossed. Surprise gave way to pleasure, then unbridled curiosity at the sight of Zach Dumas.

"He's quite a hunk," Gina said, her admiration obvious.

"He is nice-looking," Leslie agreed. If the bottom dropped out of his ranching business, Zach could easily make his living as a model. It seemed strange that a man like him, who probably had his pick of available women, had sought her out. She'd wondered how he had fared with the information she'd given him and had resigned herself to never knowing. Now, perhaps she would.

Zach caught sight of her and met her gaze with his endearing lopsided grin. She returned his smile, realizing how rusty it felt to do so.

"I hope you haven't made any definite plans for this evening," Gina said.

Trying to regain her composure, Leslie turned to face Gina. "Why?"

Gina lowered her voice. "I've seen that look before. He's not here for his health."

Leslie drew a deep breath and started forward. No doubt Zach's arrival would start Gina's tongue wagging before they passed through the double doors. She slowed her steps as she approached him. "Hi," she said.

His grin broadened. "Hi, yourself."

"Are you—"

"Are you—" They spoke at the same time, and he chuckled. "You go first."

"I was going to ask if something was wrong. I mean, most people don't come to the ER for a social visit."

He lifted one shoulder. "I didn't know where else to find you."

Zach wasn't the first man to hunt her down. Doctors, nurses, lab people, pharmacy staff and a host of other health care professionals sought her out all day long, but it was oddly exhilarating and somewhat frightening to know that Zach had made the effort. Instinctively, she sensed that her life could change, and she wasn't sure if she was ready for such an event. It had taken her so long to take the broken pieces and fit them into what she now had.

"You're lucky you caught me," she said, thinking how easily she might have missed him if she hadn't checked on Mr. Laramie or stopped to shower and change clothes.

"I am. Are you free for dinner?"

She thought of her choices—a frozen entrée eaten in front of the television, a burger in the company of co-workers who weren't in the habit of socializing with her or a dinner for two with Zach. Normally, she'd say no, but she *had* entertained the idea of changing her routine. Of course, agreeing to spend time with Zach seemed a far more daring proposition than she'd considered.

"Well," she began as she tried to decide what to do.

"Please say yes."

"Did you talk to your family?"

His grin didn't waver as he shook his head. "You won't find out unless you join me."

"That's blackmail," she protested with a smile.

"Desperation," he corrected. "So, are you free this evening?"

"As a matter of fact, I've already received an invitation," she began. The disappointment on his face was obvious, and she hurried to add, "But I left my options open."

His smile returned. "I assume that I'm a better option?"

She chuckled. "Different," she amended. "Better remains to be seen."

He turned to escort her to the door. "Shall we go?"

"Where to?"

"Armando's. That is, if you like Mexican food."

"I love it, but I've never eaten there before." Being relatively new in town, she'd heard the name mentioned but had only a vague idea of where the restaurant was located.

"Then you're in for a treat. I made reservations for six-thirty."

"Were you that sure I'd go with you?"

Color washed across his cheekbones. "Hopeful. I'm anxious to tell you what happened."

She stopped. "Then tell me now."

"If I do, you won't change your mind about your prior engagement?"

"I won't," she promised.

"I talked to my parents," he began. "The only explanation for the blood type discrepancy is that your hospital made a mistake."

"If you're trying to get on my good side, you're failing," she told him. "A mistake?"

"An error," he affirmed. "Hey, I'm not pointing a finger or finding fault, but someone in the lab had to confuse my sample with someone else's."

"While I admit that we're only human and have been less than perfect on occasion, in your case, it's highly unlikely."

"Are you one hundred percent certain?"

Since she hadn't done the test herself or seen it performed with her own eyes, she couldn't offer any guarantees. But, if she didn't have faith in the laboratory's quality, then she couldn't do her job.

"I don't have any reason *not* to believe the lab's results."

"I do. I have proof."

"Proof?" She narrowed her eyes. "What sort of proof?"

"I'll show you at dinner."

If she'd entertained any notions of wiggling out of her commitment, his remark dispelled them immediately. He'd given her enough information to draw her in, and now he had her hooked like a trout.

"You're really going to make me wait?"

"Yup," he said, clearly unrepentant. "I don't want to be late for our reservations. Come on. I'll follow you home."

Zach's arrival on her doorstep sounded too much like a date, and she wasn't ready for that. "I'll meet you."

"Where do you live?" he countered.

She listed the street name, well aware that her house and the restaurant lay in opposite directions. "In the interests of time, I'll drive myself."

"Or you can leave your car here and share a ride with me. When we're finished, I'll bring you back. If you argue, I'll consider my story off-limits until they serve dessert.''

His tone was firm, and she knew he wouldn't budge, no matter how much she begged. ''All right.''

At that moment, two people pushing a gurney out of a cubicle entered the hallway, and he pulled her aside to let them pass. As she stood plastered next to him to make room for the staff and the patient, his loose grip made her even more aware of the masculinity he exuded. His embrace seemed protective, and she found the feeling bittersweet.

It only took a few seconds for the group to move on, but time seemed to stop as she noticed his hard frame, the scent of soap and the whisper of his breath across her forehead. An instant later, he released his hold, and time started once again.

''Shall we go?''

She recovered quickly from her daydream of thinking those few seconds hadn't been nearly long enough. ''Sure.''

He guided her to a dark-blue Ford Bronco parked in an end stall. It was a late-model edition, and its exterior shone as if it had been recently washed and waxed. As he accompanied her to the passenger side where he opened her door and helped her climb aboard, she realized it had been ages since someone had shown her such a courtesy.

''Nice wheels,'' she said, hooking her seat belt before he backed into the street. ''You're obviously a horse man.''

''Why do you say that?''

''You ride one during the day and drive a Bronco at night.''

He laughed, the baritone resonating inside her. It

sounded natural, not forced, and she found herself hoping to hear it often throughout the evening. "I never thought of it like that. I generally use a pickup because I haul a lot of gear and supplies around, but my sisters refuse to ride in it."

She imagined Melinda and Kerry scolding their brother, who towered over them...and winning the argument. "What's wrong with your truck?"

"Nothing that new seats, a good cleaning and a stint in the body shop won't cure. I've used it hard over the years, so in terms of its appearance, it's in sorry shape. For my sisters' sake, I bought this a year ago."

A faint new-car smell still clung to the interior. "You must not drive it very much."

"I don't. I usually combine business and visiting my parents on my trips to town." He grinned. "Dad likes tooling around town in my old pickup. I think he gets a kick out of seeing my dirty truck parked on the same street with shiny new Beamers and Park Avenues."

"It would create a stir," she said, imagining the scene and smiling. "Your dad sounds like quite a character."

"He is," he admitted.

Armando's neon sign appeared directly ahead. Because it was a Friday night, Leslie wasn't surprised to see the parking lot full of vehicles.

Inside, Zach guided her through the crowd to the front of the line. At the sound of his name, the hostess quickly ushered them to a table for two in a corner near a huge potted cactus.

"I'm impressed," she said as he pushed in her chair before he sat down.

He glanced around the room. "Looks like any other Mexican restaurant to me."

"No, I meant the way everyone jumped when they heard your name. I've never seen people move so fast except during a code blue."

He chuckled. "Armando and I go way back. We made a mutually beneficial arrangement. He buys my beef, and I run his cooking through a taste test."

"Then you eat here a lot?"

He grinned. "Whenever I get tired of my own cooking."

The waitress arrived to take their order, and as soon as she left, Leslie leaned forward. She'd waited long enough. "We're here and we've ordered. Now tell me about your proof."

His eyes twinkled. "I wondered when you'd ask."

"Can I help it if I'm curious? So what happened?"

"Well," he began in his familiar drawl, "I talked to my parents. While some might find this difficult to believe, they've always been honest with us, so when they denied ever being unfaithful to each other, I believed them. Their life together would have been different, otherwise."

She wanted to ask him why he thought that, but he continued before she could.

"As proof that we're their children, Mom gave me this." He pulled a four-by-six-inch black-and-white picture out of his shirt pocket and handed it to her.

Leslie studied the image. She saw a woman, presumably Zach's mother, holding two babies in her arms with her husband standing beside her. Something about the snapshot tugged at her memory, but she couldn't pinpoint the exact detail.

"My mother was in labor for more than twenty-four hours," he told her. "This was taken the next day."

She couldn't deny his evidence, but it didn't explain her findings. "I don't understand."

"What's not to understand?"

She handed the photo to him. "Our results indicate—"

"That's my point. The results have to be faulty."

"I'll admit it's a possibility," she said, hating to think of someone at her facility making such a potentially life-threatening error. "So what, if anything, do you want to do?"

"I've thought about it," he said. "I said earlier that I don't want to point fingers, but the truth is, I want an explanation so we can resolve this once and for all. Tie up the loose ends, so to speak."

"I understand how you feel," she said slowly. "We can either repeat the test at West View, or I can arrange for the lab at Reno General to do the honors."

"Whichever place is best."

"Fine," she said, deciding to use another facility in order to insure unbiased results. "I'll call Reno Gen tomorrow and arrange things for you on Monday. Will that be soon enough?"

"Monday's fine."

"I know you're certain as to the outcome, but are you prepared to deal with the consequences if their lab confirms our report?"

"They won't."

For his sake, she hoped he was right. If he was wrong, then his troubles were only beginning.

"Could I see the photo again?"

"Be my guest." He pulled it out of his shirt pocket and handed it to her. His body heat had warmed the paper, causing her fingertips to tingle and her thoughts to travel along a dangerous path. ''In case you're interested,'' he added, ''I'm the handsome devil on the left.''

''I can tell,'' she teased before she grew serious. ''I feel as if I should recognize something about this picture.''

''What?''

''I'm not sure.'' The more she studied it, the more certain she became that she was staring at an important but elusive clue. What could it be? It was a basic new-mom-and-baby picture in a classic hospital-room setting.

Leslie directed her attention to the background and suddenly identified the elusive detail. ''Oh, my gosh. I have a picture just like it.''

He stared at her. ''You have a picture of my family?''

''No.'' Excitement began to grow. ''I have a photograph of my mother holding me with this same serenity prayer on the wall above the bed. We were both born at the West View Rural Clinic.''

''Really? Small world, isn't it?''

''It's more than that,'' she insisted. ''My father ran the clinic for years.''

''Then maybe he could tell us something.''

''He probably could,'' she admitted. ''But my father was Dr. Walter Keller, and he's dead.''

CHAPTER FIVE

ZACH'S surprised expression was almost comical. "Dr. Keller was your father?"

"Yes."

He snapped his fingers as if he'd finally placed her. "I saw you at his funeral a year and a half ago." His gaze grew intent, and his brow furrowed, as if he was trying to reconcile her with the woman he remembered. "You've changed."

"A person doesn't always look their best on those occasions," she said wryly.

"No, they don't, but seeing you now... You're different."

She wasn't surprised. Back then, a strong wind would have blown her away. She'd been thin, almost anorexic, and whenever she looked in a mirror, she had noticed how lifeless her eyes appeared, as if her inner spark had been extinguished.

Then again, it had been.

It had taken a long time to pull herself together, including months of therapy. She still might have shadows in her eyes, but she didn't resemble that woman any longer.

"Don't feel too bad," she said kindly as she dipped a chip into the bowl of salsa. "I've made a few changes since then, so I'm not surprised you didn't recognize me. For one thing, I cut my hair."

"That's right. You had it fixed in some sort of twist then."

"Yes, I did. I've also gained some weight." A whole dress size, in fact. She could still afford to add a few more pounds, but at least her face had lost its pinched appearance.

"Had you been ill when your dad died?"

"I'd been going through a tough time," she admitted, her gaze not quite meeting his as she spoke. "My husband and son had died about six months earlier. I was still dealing with that when I got word about my father."

"I'm sorry about your family. Was it an accident?"

"Yes." She dipped another chip to avoid going into detail. "Did you know my father well?"

Zach recognized a subject change when he heard one. If she didn't want to talk about certain aspects of her life, he would respect her wishes. At least he understood her fragile appearance at the funeral. If a similar series of tragedies had struck him, he'd have looked like death warmed over, too.

"He was a great guy," he said simply. "Dr. Keller and my parents were close friends. He'd drop in at least once a week to visit. He wouldn't stay long, but he always managed to put in an appearance."

"Really?"

"He loved my mom's pecan pie. But then, you probably knew that."

"Actually, I didn't. I didn't see much of him. He divorced my mother when I was small. After we moved to California, I only saw him once in a while. He visited on my birthday and Christmas, and of course, he attended all of my graduations from high school through medical school."

"Distance makes it hard to stay a part of a child's life. I'm lucky my ex-wife moved to Vegas. At least I'm in the same state as my boys."

"You have children?"

"Two sons. They're twins. Keith and Kenny are ten."

"You must miss them."

"It's been three years since the divorce, but at times it seems like yesterday. Melinda says I work too hard." He shrugged. "A man has to pass the days somehow."

"How often do you see them?"

"Every other weekend. They're supposed to spend June and July with me, but Monica enrolled them in different sports camps. I'm trying to convince her to change her mind, but if the boys want to go, I won't stand in their way."

"You hope they'll want to come here, though."

She'd read his mind. "Actually, I want them to *live* here."

"Do you think you'll ever get custody?"

"I don't know, but you can be sure I won't do anything to jeopardize my chances. They already love the ranch almost as much as I do. After all, it's their legacy, just as it's mine. Unfortunately, Monica, my ex-wife, never understood that. She hated the long hours I put in, never accepting or wanting to accept the reality that cattle and the weather operate on their own schedules. Her catering business is giving her a taste of it, though."

"So she left because you weren't paying enough attention to her?"

"That and the fact that she decided to let our accountant fill her evenings."

"I see. He obviously wasn't teaching her your book-keeping system."

"The only figure he had his eye on was my wife's." This was the first time he could remember talking about that period of his life without despair gnawing at the pit of his stomach. "The worst part about it was her dishonesty. Their relationship had gone on for quite a while before I found out. I'd told her before we got married that the ranch would take a lot of my time because I didn't intend to be an absentee owner and rely on my foreman to handle my business. It didn't bother her at first, but as the years went by, it did."

She touched his arm in a comforting gesture, but instead, Zach found her caress immensely arousing. "I'm sorry."

"It takes two to tango," he said. "I should have seen the signs, but I didn't. I'm as much at fault as she is."

"Maybe. I imagine that ranching is like medicine. It isn't always a nine-to-five job."

Her insight was refreshing. He liked Leslie Keller Hall more and more with each passing moment. Of course, he couldn't tell her that. He wasn't sure where he wanted to go with this, but spending time with a woman who wasn't fixated on herself was like enjoying a breath of fresh air after mucking out the barn.

"Exactly," he answered. "Fortunately, I had an excellent attorney and I managed to keep my portion of the Twin Bar Ranch out of her hands for the boys."

"You are lucky. A lot of guys lose everything. Anyway, I hope everything works out the way you want."

He cleared his throat and shifted positions. "I hope so, too. Did you ever spend time with Walter here in Nevada?" The closeness of the moment seemed to break, and she withdrew her hand. The loss only made him crave her touch.

"When I was younger," she said. "Later on, I was busy with school and a part-time job and didn't visit."

"What sort of job did you have? Wait, don't tell me. Let me guess. Let's see." He gazed at her and pictured a younger, coltish version of the woman across from him. "You shelved books in the library."

"I spent enough time there, but you're wrong."

"All right. Were you a waitress?"

She shook her head.

"A clerk in a department store."

She chuckled. "No. Do you give up?"

Zach loved her smile and the sound of her laughter. He suspected that she didn't do either frequently, and he was glad to cajole both out of her. "Yeah."

"I worked at a zoo."

"A zoo?"

She nodded. "I did everything from feed the animals to mow the grass at the park. Fortunately, the director understood my aversion to reptiles and gave the snake duty to one of the other kids."

"A zoo." He shook his head. "I never would have guessed."

"I didn't think you would. At one time, I even considered becoming a veterinarian."

"Why didn't you? Or did the snakes scare you off?"

"I hate to admit it, but yes, they did. I figured that humans were basically a different type of animal, so I switched my emphasis to medical school. My mother wasn't happy, but Dad was thrilled."

"I'll bet. With your dad gone, what brought you to Reno?"

"I needed a change. Fortunately, West View Hospital

had an opening, and since I inherited his house, it seemed the perfect place to start over.''

He met her gaze and, raising his bottle of beer, said, ''Here's to a new beginning.''

''And to new friends.'' She clicked her glass against his Coors Light before sipping hers.

''The town has changed a lot since you were a kid,'' he observed as the waitress chose that moment to serve their plates of steaming chili rellenos and enchiladas.

''Tell me about it,'' she said woefully as she began eating. ''It's a completely different town from what I remember.''

''The area has grown. I remember your dad's clinic and how the suburbs sprang up all around it almost overnight.''

''He told me. He felt terrible because he had to struggle to meet the demands of the growing population. When the hospital board approached him about buying his clinic and turning it into a hospital, he was ready to let go.''

''The responsibilities had to be great. I remember how people were worried that he'd retire, but he never did. Mom and Dad speculated that he would, but whenever they asked him about it, he'd always grin and say, 'Maybe next year.'''

''I'd suggested it myself several times,'' she said with a reminiscent smile, ''and he said the same thing. I finally realized why he never completely quit. He needed his patients as much as they needed him.''

Zach thought of his own reasons for working so hard. ''I imagine you're right. Work is what kept me sane.''

''Everyone needs a reason to get up in the morning.'' While they ate, they chatted about the changes in Reno over the years and traded memories of the city from their childhood.

Once Leslie finished her meal, she pushed her plate aside and dabbed at her mouth. "That was delicious. Give my compliments to Armando the next time you see him."

"I will." After settling the bill and leaving a generous tip at the table, Zach ushered Leslie to the door. "How about a drink before I take you back?"

"Thanks, but it's getting late, and you have to drive home."

"The ranch is only thirty miles from here," he said. "But it has been a long day." Although he didn't want the evening to end, he didn't want to wear out his welcome, either.

Night had nearly fallen, and the streetlights had started to glow as he drove her to the hospital.

"I'm parked in the doctors' lot," she told him. "Mine is the fourth car from the end."

Zach rolled to a stop behind her white Grand Am. "I'll follow you home."

"That isn't necessary."

"No, but I want to, so I will."

"I can drive across town by myself."

"I know. Just humor me, okay?"

Her smile did funny things to his heart rate. "Okay."

She slid out of the passenger side of his car and got in her own. Zach pulled ahead so she could back out of her parking space, then followed her across town. He wondered if his parents knew that Walter's daughter had moved into his home. He'd have fun relaying information that the senior citizens' gossip hot line had missed.

He also wondered if his parents had ever met Leslie.

If they hadn't, he intended to rectify the oversight. If all went well, they'd be seeing a lot of her in the days ahead.

Fifteen minutes after leaving the hospital, he arrived at the two-story house he remembered. By the time she drove into the detached garage, shut off the engine and got out, Zach had parked his Bronco on her driveway and was leaning indolently against the front grill.

"I made it, safe and sound," she said lightly.

"I didn't have any doubts. Will I see you again?"

She hesitated, as if unsure of her answer. "Reno isn't *that* big. You also know where I work."

"I wasn't referring to a professional visit."

"I didn't think you were." She drew a deep breath. "I shouldn't say this, but I know you value honesty. As much as I enjoy your company, I'm not ready to jump into the dating scene."

A pregnant pause filled the night air while satisfaction unfurled inside him. "Then you felt it, too?" he asked softly.

"Felt what?" Her tone was guarded, as if admitting the experience made it an undeniable fact.

"That sense of familiarity. You're easy to talk to."

"Oh, that." She waved one hand in dismissal. "Yes, well, it's probably because I've learned how to be a good listener. I'm a doctor, you know."

He straightened, then closed the distance between them until the warmth emanating from her body seemed like an embrace. "I hate to ruin your theory, but believe me, it's not because you're a doctor."

"I don't know what else it could possibly be. Medicine is my life, just like it was for my father."

He heard the note of near desperation in her denial. She was ready to bolt, and if he wanted this discussion to continue, he needed to calm her fears. "I understand."

"Do you?"

"Sure, but even he had a personal life." According to his parents, Walter spent most of his days, and nights, working, but Zach didn't share that detail. She didn't need more ammunition.

"Granted, we both have issues," he continued, "*personal* issues. But aren't there times when you just want to be with someone?"

"We're both with people all day long."

"I can tell you haven't hung around a bunch of range hands before," he said dryly. "Being with them isn't the same as being with a lady. Sometimes a fellow needs a little female companionship to smooth his rough edges. Don't you ever want to spend a few hours with a person who will let you be Leslie Hall and not Dr. Hall?"

Her mouth tightened. "Okay, I get your point."

"So, to repeat myself, will I see you again?"

"Why do I get the feeling that no matter what I say, you'll do what you want?"

It struck him how quickly she'd learned to read his character. "Because you're an intuitive, intelligent lady."

"Compliments will get you nowhere fast."

"I call 'em like I see 'em. Are you going to answer my question or not?"

"Speaking as one *friend* to another, since you know where I live, I imagine you will see me again. Once in a while."

Picking up her subtle emphasis on the word *friend,* he recognized the limits she placed upon them. He'd honor her wishes, for now. "Then it's settled. Now, about my blood work on Monday—"

"I'll call Tuesday with your results. If you'd like, though, you could just ask the lab to mail or fax a copy directly to you."

"I'll wait for your call," he decided. "If the lab at West View has made an error, you'll want to lop off a few heads."

"Yes, I will." She held out her hand. "Thanks again for dinner and the pleasant evening."

He wanted to pull her close and kiss her gently, but the timing was wrong. She wasn't a woman to be rushed, and if waiting insured success, then he'd wait.

To his surprise, she stretched on tiptoe and kissed his cheek. The feather-light caress of her lips on his skin, the aroma of spices teasing his nose and the feel of her breasts brushing against his chest nearly undid his good intentions. The moment ended as quickly as it had occurred, and it left him wanting more. Much more.

"Good night," she said softly, before she spun around and hurried up the porch steps.

Zach remained frozen as he heard her insert the key into the lock. His body seemed branded by her touch, and heat surged through him until he felt as if he'd combust. Tuesday seemed a lifetime away.

"How was your weekend?" Betty asked on Tuesday morning. Having enjoyed three days off, she arrived at work rested and relaxed and appeared more bubbly than usual.

"My weekend?" Leslie asked, her attention jolted from the patient notes she was reviewing. Monday had been as hectic as Friday, and today was shaping itself into a carbon copy. Staff members were bustling around, phones were constantly ringing, and Leslie was trying to juggle her paperwork, answer questions from the staff and diagnose patients at the same time.

"Yeah. You know, the period that begins Friday after work and ends Monday morning?"

"Oh. It was nice. I got a lot of work done around the house." Actually, she'd accomplished everything she'd planned to do over the next two weeks. Zach's request to see her again had sent her into a flurry of exhaustive activity. Working nonstop had helped take her mind off him and her impulsive kiss, although at odd moments, thoughts of him returned with a vengeance. Still, her father's house shone like a new penny, and the flower beds were ready for planting.

"Did you have a nice time on your date Friday night?"

The hospital network was clearly more efficient than the AP News Service. It wouldn't surprise her if Gina was Betty's buddy, too.

"It wasn't a date," Leslie said. "A friend came by before I left the hospital and asked me to dinner."

"Anyone I know?" Betty asked coyly.

"Zach Dumas."

"Ah," she said knowingly. "I figured he'd be back."

"What are you talking about?"

"Oh, nothing. It's just I made a bet with myself that you hadn't seen the last of him, and it looks like I won. So what did you do?"

"We ate out and then I went home. End of story."

"No nightcap?" Betty sounded horrified.

"Not even a glass of water." She was proud of herself for resisting the temptation. From the moment his twin headlight beams hit her rearview mirror on the way home, she decided against it. Asking him in would have sent the wrong signals. Yet after she'd gone inside, she'd wanted to watch him drive away from behind the curtains, but she hadn't. It would have been far too easy to indulge her impulse to run out and beg him to stay a little longer.

Betty shook her head. "Look. You may be older and have a medical degree under your belt, but bagging a fellow is my area of expertise. You're going about this all wrong."

"I don't *want* to bag a fellow."

"You don't want Zach Dumas? Holy cow, Leslie. He and his brother are every woman's fantasy."

"Not this woman's." Denying it didn't change the fact that Betty was right.

"Well, I suppose being a widow and all, you're not ready to rush into anything," Betty conceded. "That doesn't mean you can't have a little fun in the meantime."

"I'm not ready for fun, either."

"Having fun is a state of mind. Did you two click? You know, no pregnant pauses, no moments of wishing you were somewhere else *with* someone else?"

Betty's definition was apt, but Leslie didn't want her to know the details. The grapevine would have them engaged before her shift ended. "I didn't throw my drink in his face, and we left on speaking terms. Does that answer your question?"

"No, but answer this. Will you go out with him again?"

"Maybe—if I'm free."

Betty's face brightened. "I get it. You're playing hard to get."

"I'm not playing anything." She handed her the

chart. "As soon as the pharmacy delivers these pills, give them to the patient and send him on his way."

"Yes, ma'am."

She ignored Betty's sarcastic tone. At least she'd given the nurse a task to focus on instead of the subject of Zach Dumas. Whether she wanted it to happen or not, whether she called it sparks or electricity or just plain magnetic attraction between two people who'd loved and lost, she and Zach had connected.

Because of that very connection, she was leery about seeing him again. He'd been far too comfortable to be around, and so willing to just be friends that it unnerved her. During her brief kiss of gratitude, she'd felt his arousal, and for the first time since Michael and Brandon's deaths, she'd experienced a hormonal surge herself. Emotionally, though, she wasn't ready to take such a monumental step.

Then again, why was she worried about something that probably wouldn't happen? With his busy life and her rather erratic schedule, at best they would be passing acquaintances. Eventually, he'd find another woman who would give him the companionship he craved.

Companionship.

Ever since he'd mentioned being with someone who would let her be Leslie and not just a doctor, she realized how badly she wanted that very thing. With his talk about loneliness, Zach had instantly changed the way she viewed her life. As she tackled her chores, the house she'd thought of as her refuge suddenly seemed like an empty cavern, and the rooms had mocked her as she passed by. The building had been designed for a family, not for one person to rattle around in like a marble in a quart jar.

Why hadn't her father sold his home after the divorce? She knew how tough it was to walk into a place where sorrow had replaced wonderful memories. Considering how much time he devoted to his practice, her father should have moved into an efficiency apartment, as she had.

The answer to her question came with a flash. Her father had carried hope in his heart—hope that one day his family might be restored, and the walls would resonate with the sound of laughter. If that never happened, he could imagine his grandchildren filling those empty spaces.

She didn't have that luxury. The death of her husband and son had erased every one of her dreams, which was why she couldn't bear to stay in the place where they'd happily anticipated the future.

"Dr. Hall?" The day shift ward clerk, a nondescript woman in her mid fifties, approached her. "This fax came for you."

"Thanks." Leslie took the page and immediately noticed the letterhead. Reno General Hospital.

The body of the report held only a few short words, and as she read them, she tensed. Someone had certainly made a mistake.

A major mistake.

ZACH'S CELL PHONE barely finished its first warble before he answered. Thanks to one of his purebred Angus cows suffering through a difficult birth, he'd already missed one call. He hoped it hadn't been Leslie's, but if it had, surely she would try again. She'd promised to contact him today, and it was already half past six.

"Hey, Zach." Melinda's familiar voice sounded in his ear. "What's going on?"

"Work," he said shortly, wanting to get his sister off

the line as soon as possible. "Did you want something in particular or did you just decide to visit?"

"Ooh," she crooned. "Someone's grumpy. Having a bad day?"

"I'm expecting a call."

"Oh." Her tone became serious. "Then I won't keep you. I wanted to know if you've heard from Zane."

"I wish. Why? Has something come up?"

"His life insurance policy is due, and he hasn't transferred enough money into his checking account to cover the premium. I hate to let it lapse, all things considered."

Zach agreed. With his brother hightailing it to parts unknown to do whatever, a life insurance policy was a necessity. "How much do you need?"

Melinda named a figure. "If we want to renew this, I have to pay the fee by the end of the week."

"I'll write a check and bring it when I come over," he told her.

"Thanks, Zach. I didn't want to bother Dad because I know how worried he is. I knew I could count on you."

Zach hit the end button as he added this task to his mental list. His brother wouldn't come home soon enough to suit him.

Every other day he kept the phone in his pickup, but today he carried it on his belt. He was as eager to hear Leslie's voice as he was to hear his test results.

Zach walked out of the barn and headed for the house, where his overflowing in basket demanded his attention. Although he'd rather do anything than add endless columns of numbers, it hadn't been that long since concentrating on figures had kept him from bending his elbow with a whiskey bottle to numb the pain.

As he strode along the driveway, his attention honed in on the white Grand Am parked in front of his house. He only knew of one person who owned such a vehicle, and he immediately quickened his pace. A smile spread across his face as soon as he saw her seated in the porch swing that hung suspended from the rafters, and he bounded up the steps two at a time.

"Leslie. What a nice surprise."

She stopped swinging and stood. "I received your results today."

"You didn't need to drive all the way out here," he said, "although I'm glad you did."

She brushed a stray curl out of her eye. "I thought this news was best delivered in person."

"So someone *did* make a mistake," he said, pleased to be proven correct.

"Someone did," she admitted. "But it wasn't the lab."

Her serious tone and the worry in her dark eyes sent his stomach dropping to his toes. "It wasn't?"

She shook her head. "You're still an A positive."

He couldn't believe it, even after she handed over the document in her hand. "See for yourself," she urged.

The letters blurred on the page. "Then it's true."

"I'm afraid so. You can't be your father's biological son."

CHAPTER SIX

LESLIE FELT utterly helpless as Zach perched on the porch rail to read the report again. He'd believed wholeheartedly that the lab had made a mistake, and it wasn't easy watching his faith in the world he knew crumble into dust.

"I'm sorry, Zach."

"It's not your fault. It's just hard to believe that I'm not the person I thought I was."

"Of course you are—you're the same man you were a few minutes ago," Leslie insisted as she took his hand. "You have the same likes and dislikes, the same abilities and the same character. That part hasn't changed."

"True," he admitted. "I always wondered which side of the family Zane and my talents came from, and we joked about it for years. Obviously we're from an entirely different gene pool." He hesitated. "I wish I knew what happened."

"Your parents haven't been hiding any information from you," Leslie said. "For them to use this picture as proof, they clearly believe that you and Zane are their flesh-and-blood sons. Since you aren't, we have to consider other possibilities."

"If you're going to say the stork brought us, forget it."

"Maybe not the stork," she said slowly as she began

to pace, ''but you and your brother could have been switched.''

''Switched? That sounds more far-fetched than the other ideas you've had.''

''Perhaps, but it's highly possible that you and your brother may have gone home with the wrong set of parents.''

''Aren't you reaching a bit?''

''No more than when you thought your mother had an affair or that your parents adopted you. It's a logical deduction.''

''You're telling me that a couple wouldn't know if they delivered one baby and went home with two?''

She tapped her foot in apparent exasperation. ''You and Zane are identical, right?''

''Yes.''

''Then both of you had to be switched.''

''Someone else who had twin boys went home with the wrong set. Is that what you're telling me?''

''Yes.''

''What's the likelihood of two women arriving at your father's clinic thirty-eight years ago, each delivering male twins on the same day?''

''I'm not a statistician. I'm merely mentioning it as something to consider.''

He rubbed the back of his neck and flexed his shoulders as he rose. For a few seconds, he simply stared into the distance, not saying a word. She was almost afraid he'd walk away, but then he spoke. ''How do we prove your theory?''

She hadn't expected him to ask for proof. ''I don't know that we can,'' she said honestly. ''The next question is, do you really want to dredge up the past and ruin everyone's life?''

"For all we know, the other innocent parties are going through the same turmoil," he said. "If someone at your father's clinic made a mistake..."

The thought had crossed her mind, but hearing it articulated didn't make the idea easier to swallow. "If someone did make such a monumental error, how will exposing it at this late date help matters?"

"Someone has to know the truth."

"Who?" she demanded to know. "My father is dead, and his staff could be dead, too, or in nursing homes. Are you willing to trust the memory of someone who doesn't know what day of the week it is? Searching through the records could take months. Years."

"I'm not going anywhere."

"Regardless of what happened and who was responsible, this isn't something that can be undone. What will you gain in the process? Is the information worth the risk of destroying the family you have?" She didn't want to see his family torn apart, as hers had been.

"I'm not out to destroy anyone's life. Searching for the truth has nothing to do with how satisfied or dissatisfied I am with my parents, and yes, I still think of Eleanor and Hamilton as my parents. I'm not looking to replace them."

"Then why dig up things better left forgotten?"

"Because I need to know," he said simply. "I want a sense of who I am and where I came from. I'm curious about what my birth parents look like, how they talk, what they do for a living. I want to know their talents and their personalities. For all I know, they passed on a disease that is a ticking time bomb, or one that I'll pass down to my boys.

"This is a family mystery, *my* family mystery, and I

want it solved. Because your father could be involved, I'd think you'd want to find out what happened, too.''

"I do, but not at the risk of tarnishing his spotless reputation.'' The news media would descend like vultures on this story, and while delving into her father's past, an enterprising reporter with a nose for dirt could ferret out her secrets, as well.

"I have to know, Leslie, but I can't dump this on my parents or my sisters. You're the only one who can help me discover the truth. Once I learn what it is, I'll decide what to do.''

Seeing the resolve in his eyes, she knew she couldn't refuse. Because he valued honesty, his desire to discover the truth wasn't surprising, and who better to help him than her? Still, becoming his partner in this endeavor was extremely disconcerting. Investigating would take hours—hours most likely spent in his company.

On the other hand, she would reap some benefits, too. She'd never been close to her father, and after losing her husband and son, she regretted that fact more than ever. This could easily be an opportunity to learn what sort of man her father had been.

"I'll help you,'' she said reluctantly, "but only if you promise that whatever we find will never go beyond the two of us unless we both agree.''

"I have to tell Zane. He's part of this, too.''

"Fine. This stays among the three of us.''

Before she had a chance to think of possible repercussions, Zach closed the distance between them in two short strides. "Thank you,'' he said. "I'm grateful.''

She managed a smile. "Just don't be disappointed if we can't find the answers you want. After thirty-eight years, the trail is probably stone cold.''

"As long as I know we gave it our best shot, I can live with the outcome. I appreciate what you're doing for me."

Without warning, he kissed her. As kisses went, it was rather sweet, but in the space of a heartbeat, everything changed. What had started as a friendly gesture became powerful enough to take her breath away. He raised his head, and from the stunned expression on his face, she knew the experience had been mutual.

Suddenly, she found herself locked in his embrace with his mouth hovering dangerously close to hers. She could have turned away, but instead, she clutched his shoulders and silently begged for more. He may have intended the first kiss to be platonic, but the gleam in his eye suggested this one would be far, far different.

He didn't disappoint her. His lips moved against hers, and her worries faded away as if they'd become inconsequential. His arm pressed her against his full length, and she felt the hard planes of his body. She, too, began to explore, moving her hands over his shoulders and across his back, which long hours of backbreaking labor had turned into toned muscle.

The fragrances of fresh air and hard work mingled with his unique scent in a most pleasant combination. His touch was like water, her body a meadow during the height of the dry season. He gave life to all the arid places inside her, allowing emotions she'd long suppressed to sprout instantly and grow until Zach occupied every nook and cranny of her mind.

His hand slid underneath her sweater. Goose bumps rose, but she didn't know if they were due to the cool air against her bare skin or her reaction to the gentle caress by work-roughened fingers. An ache began to build like summer storm clouds gathering together until they gained enough momentum to unleash their fury.

In the distance, several cows bawled. The noise broke the spell surrounding them, and he slowly adjusted her sweater before he released her. "If you expect me to apologize, I won't. I'm not sorry at all."

How could she expect him to apologize when she'd encouraged him? All she could say in her defense was that she'd temporarily lost her good sense. She began to pace as she attempted to sort out her tangled thoughts. "This certainly complicates matters."

She hadn't realized she'd spoken aloud until he asked, "How?"

Where should she begin? "I'll admit there's chemistry between us, but it can't go anywhere."

"Why not?"

His question stopped her in her tracks. How could she explain it? For those few minutes, she'd felt so cherished, but once he learned about her sordid past, the light in his eyes would dim. She'd rather not raise her hopes only to have them dashed at some future date.

"You've already mentioned how we both have issues to work out," she reminded him.

"Yeah, but you can't tell me that you don't have a few empty spots inside you waiting to be filled."

"My career is filling those nicely, thank you," she said primly. "As for those empty spots you're referring to, I barely survived losing the people I loved. I'm not ready to risk going through the same experience."

"I understand, but—"

"You simply can't kiss me again."

He was a picture of innocence as he folded his arms across his chest. "Ever?"

"Ever."

"Why not?"

"It's too distracting. We have to focus our attention on the job at hand, which is searching for your birth parents' identity."

A lazy grin crawled across his face. "I distract you?"

She ignored his question. Replying would only increase his already swelled head. "If you want my help, then you have to play by my rules. Otherwise, you're on your own."

He straightened to his full height and calmly met her gaze. "Don't get your stethoscope in a knot. If that's the way you want it, then I won't kiss you."

"It is."

His mouth twitched as if he were holding back a smile, and his eyes filled with a predatory gleam. Suddenly, she realized what she'd done. She'd issued a challenge that any red-blooded male would accept without question.

"All right," he said. "I'll play along." Before she could breathe a sigh of relief, he added, "Just remember one thing. Rules are made to be broken."

His intentions were crystal clear. She would have to be on guard at all times.

"How about a cup of coffee?" he asked.

He obviously realized that she'd figured out his strategy and decided to let the subject rest. "I really should be driving back to town."

"Do you have other plans?" he asked.

Pinned under his gaze, she had to tell the truth. She suspected he was a master at recognizing feeble excuses. "N-no."

He opened the screen door. "Good, because after news like this, I could use a jolt of caffeine."

Her gaze darted toward the stairs, then to him. "I really should go."

"We have to figure out our game plan," he reminded her. "We might as well enjoy a cup of coffee and a piece of pie while we're hashing out the details. Unless you haven't eaten dinner yet."

It seemed churlish to refuse. "I grabbed a sandwich before I came, but coffee would be nice." Then, thinking of some of the turns she'd navigated to find the Twin Bar Ranch, she added, "I can't stay too late, though. I'm not sure I'll find my way home in the dark."

"Where did you get directions?" he asked.

"My boss. Dr. Norman Rice. Maybe you've heard of him?"

"Can't say that I have. I would have thought that, being a doctor, you don't need a boss."

She laughed. "I'm a hospital employee like everyone else. The medical staff has its own hierarchy, and I'm low man on the totem pole. Even after my probation ends, I'll still answer to him."

"I didn't realize it worked that way." He led the way into the kitchen.

Leslie received impressions of rich colors, wood and the lingering scent of simmering beef as she followed him. There, she gazed at her surroundings in awe. It was a kitchen she'd always dreamed of having. Cherry wood cabinets. An oversize island with four bar stools on one side and pots hanging above it. A china cupboard and an antique pie safe. All created a casual and homey atmosphere. Yellow gingham curtains hung at the two windows overlooking the west lawn and the south window in the breakfast nook.

"This is lovely," she exclaimed.

"Thanks. When I was a kid, we had a table that seated twelve, but after my divorce, I hated sitting at it by myself. Because we have a formal dining room, I sold it and installed the island."

"Then you grew up here?"

"This was my dad's ranch. After he had his heart attack, he decided to retire and so he divided the property. I took the front half since it was better suited to cattle and the few horses I raise. Zane wanted the back half for his Arabians. The land's more rugged but it butts up against the foothills. His wife liked the scenery."

"Then Zane built his house?"

"As a matter of fact, no. A cavalry unit was stationed in this area in the eighteen hundreds, and their quarters were on what became Zane's section of land. The men built their post out of native stone, like my house, so the buildings held up rather well. The interior was a completely different story. Zane had to remodel from top to bottom in order to make it livable."

He grinned. "As Dad always said, 'Waste not, want not,' and it seemed a shame to tear down those structures when they played an important part in local history. If you want to see the rest of the house, I'll show you around while we're waiting for the coffee."

"I'd like that."

"What's your preference?" he asked, measuring grounds into the basket. "Weak, or strong enough to hold a spoon?"

"Somewhere in between. May I help?"

He pointed to a cupboard near the sink. "Mugs are on the bottom shelf. Spoons are in the drawer."

Leslie removed the dishes and found the cutlery

while he poured water into the reservoir. "Do you raise anything besides cattle?"

"I breed a few quarter horses, but they're more of a hobby. I concentrate on purebred Angus and Romagnola registered cattle. The Romagnolas are low-fat beeves, and their bulls produce calves with more meat and less waste when they're used with commercial animals."

"Then you sell the bulls?"

"Well, now," he drawled. "I'll sell whatever the buyer wants. Heifers, bred cows, semen, you name it. We'll even lease our bulls if someone can't afford to buy one."

"You must be very busy."

"It fills my day." He leaned against the counter and crossed his arms as steam began to rise from the coffeemaker. "Enough about cattle. I want to hear your ideas on how we should find my birth parents."

"Oh, no, you don't," she protested. "You promised me a tour first."

"I can't go back on my word, now, can I?"

Because the house was a sprawling single-level structure, he led her down the hallway from the kitchen to the four bedrooms. "It's nothing fancy," he warned. "I spend most of my time in the kitchen or my office."

"Do you take care of the house yourself?" she asked, noticing how immaculate the surfaces appeared and wondering when he found the time.

"A cleaning service comes twice a month," he admitted. "They probably wouldn't need to clean that often, but I'd hate for my mom to see her former home turned into a pigpen. She worked hard to train the four of us to pick up after ourselves, and I don't want her to think she failed."

His consideration for his mother's feelings touched her.

"This first room used to be a combination of Mom's sewing room and my dad's office," he said. "I turned it into my den."

Leslie noticed the state-of-the-art computer sitting on top of the cherry wood desk, where piles of papers lay in disarray. A fax machine and phone rested on the matching credenza, and a high-backed leather chair faced the door, as if its occupant had left abruptly.

On the wall hung a variety of diplomas and several groupings of framed pencil sketches. One arrangement showed toddlers playing, while another set displayed horses and still another depicted the buildings on his farm. "What lovely artwork," she exclaimed as she moved in for a closer look. "Who's the artist?"

A scrawled *Z. Dumas* in the lower right-hand corner caught her eye. "*You're* the one who drew these?"

He dug his fingers in his pockets and grinned. "Yup."

"Why, these are wonderful."

"Thanks."

She pointed to the set of buildings. "I recognize the house and the barn, but what's this?"

"The cavalry quarters I told you about. I drew that before Zane remodeled them."

Leslie moved to the three matted sketches of children. Two were of twin boys sitting on the porch swing, and one featured a little boy and a girl playing in a sandbox. "I assume these two are Melinda's children."

"Yeah. The twins are mine. Keith and Kenny. They were five at the time."

"These are absolutely fantastic. You have a remarkable gift."

"Thanks."

"Do you have any others?"

"They're in every room, but most of my work is still in sketchbooks."

"I'm envious. I can hardly draw stick people. Would you draw something for me?"

"Sure. What would you like?"

"I don't know. I'll have to think about it."

"Here's the room I shared with Zane." He opened the door, and she saw the twin beds with their matching red comforters. It was a typical boy's room, complete with airplanes, footballs and horses. A photo of Zach and his boys at a shooting gallery stood on the dresser. She recognized the resemblance.

"We took that picture about three years ago at a carnival in Vegas," he mentioned. "Our last family vacation."

His smile dimmed, and she felt his pain. How deeply it must hurt to want to be a major part of his sons' lives and to receive only crumbs. She motioned around the room. "They seem to be typical boys."

"They are." The note of pride had returned to his voice. "Melinda and Kerry shared the next room. I use it as a spare. My room is down the hall."

It seemed rather intimate to peek in his bedroom. A hat hung on one post of the four-poster bed, and the walls were covered with more of Zach's sketches. What caught her eye, though, was the quilt covering the bed.

"I like your quilt," she said, stepping inside to run her hand across the stitches of the design. "I don't recognize the pattern."

"My grandmother made it for us as a wedding gift. I think it was something she designed on her own."

"It's beautiful."

"I like it, too. I just wish I had two of them so I could pass one down to each of my boys."

"Maybe you can contact a quilt guild. I'm sure those ladies would love to piece something together for you."

"Yeah, but it wouldn't be the same as having a relative sewing it."

"I suppose not." A keen sense of disappointment struck Leslie. While people might someday purchase her own hand-stitched quilts at premium prices and appreciate both the quality and the time involved, none would ever feel that connection of an ancestor's past meeting the present.

"Next stop is the living room," he said.

He'd dispelled her maudlin moment. Regardless of what happened to her quilts a hundred years from now, at this point, they'd helped restore her sanity. "Lead on."

She entered the area she'd passed through briefly on her way to the kitchen. It, too, was large, but the stone fireplace on the east wall drew her attention. Huge wooden beams stretched across the ceiling, and a wrought-iron chandelier hung in the center.

An antique mahogany rolltop desk stood near the doorway, but the rest of the furniture was modern. A brown leather sofa and two recliners were grouped together on the braided area rug in a cozy arrangement. A pewter statue of a rider on a bucking horse stood on the coffee table.

As in the other rooms, Zach's drawings lined the walls. Her gaze followed them until she caught sight of a large cabinet with glass doors in the far corner. The contents made her stiffen, and a sick feeling rose in her stomach as she counted six rifles and two handguns.

She breathed deeply and willed her heart rate to slow.

She shouldn't have been surprised to see the weapons. With wild animals coming down from the mountains in search of food, people needed guns for protection. Still, the knowledge didn't make it easier for her to accept their presence.

"I hope you keep that locked," she said, trying to hide her aversion behind a teasing tone. It didn't work. Her words sounded sharp, and she noticed Zach's expression become speculative.

"Always," he said. "I store the ammunition in a separate place, and the locks for each require different keys. I keep them on me at all times."

"Someone could break the glass."

"It's bulletproof," he said. "Cost me an arm and a leg, but with Melinda's kids and my boys around, it was worth it. You don't like guns, do you?"

She shrugged, trying to appear nonchalant. "I've seen what they do to the human body, and it isn't a pretty sight."

"I don't imagine it is." He tipped his head, then said, "I think the coffee's ready."

"Great." She was eager to leave this room before she said or did anything to pique his interest more than she already had. "I could use a cup."

"So where should we start looking?" he asked as he filled her mug and set it on the island. "Ask the state bureau of vital statistics to find out who was born in this county on our birth date?"

Leslie balanced herself on a bar stool and stirred a spoon of sugar into the brew. "I don't know if they're capable of doing that type of search. And even if they could, I'm not sure they would. I'd think there would be a local record, but that may not be the case. Files get lost or destroyed."

"Since the hospital took over from the clinic, would they have any of the information we're looking for?"

"Actually, most—if not all—of the Keller clinic's documents are stored in my basement."

"They are?" His voice held undisguised excitement.

"I found them after I moved into my father's house. I don't know how they're organized, but I can tell you there are boxes and boxes of patient charts. He practiced for more than forty years, and I'd say there are hundreds, *thousands,* of medical files."

"Would any of his staff still be around?"

"I doubt it. As I've said, they're probably dead or in nursing homes. I didn't know any of them." Leslie only knew the name of her father's nurse, Barbara Memovich, and she had left town after her father died. Because Barbara had been responsible for her parents' divorce, Leslie hadn't cared to keep track of her.

"Surely he has employment records, W-2s, that sort of information, on file."

Leslie shrugged. "We'll have to look."

"When can we get started?"

She thought a moment. "I'm off duty tomorrow afternoon. I'll start poking around."

"I may be able to get away then, too."

"You don't have to," she began.

"Oh, yes, I do. This is my mystery, and I'm not going to let you have all the fun."

"I don't know how much fun it will be to poke around a dusty basement."

"Fun. Work." He gestured wildly. "It's a matter of semantics. What time do you want to begin?"

"Maybe you should wait until I sort through the boxes and see what records I have," she said.

"If you think I'll sit back and wait for you to do the work, then don't."

"What about your cattle?"

"My foreman knows what to do, and if not, he can call me." He raised one eyebrow. "Will you pick a time or shall I just show up on your doorstep?"

Accepting the inevitable, she said, "I should be home by one."

"I'll be there by one-thirty."

Leslie noticed the sun had appeared in the west window and realized the mountain range would soon block it completely. "It's late. I really have to go. Thanks again for the coffee."

"My pleasure." He accompanied her to her car, guiding her with his hand at the small of her back.

His touch sent a shiver of pleasure down her spine, and she alternated between wanting him to remove his palm and wanting him to pull her into his embrace. She should have told him to keep his hands to himself, but she'd only stipulated that he couldn't kiss her.

Suddenly, she wished she hadn't made that rule at all.

CHAPTER SEVEN

"WHERE do we begin?"

Standing at the bottom of Leslie's basement steps the next afternoon, Zach surveyed the task ahead of them. Boxes, stacked chest-high, filled three-fourths of the unfinished room. The surfaces were grimy with undisturbed dust, and a musty smell greeted him. Sunshine streamed in through two small windows on the west side of the house, illuminating the motes suspended in the air.

"Wherever we want," she said wryly, wrinkling her nose.

Zach whistled. "I knew your father had a long and busy career, but I never dreamed we'd have to sort through this much." He examined the outside of one box. "It doesn't look like anything's labeled, either."

"That won't make our job any easier," she said. "When the staff closed his office after his death, I thought they would have filed things in some sort of system."

He took off the lid and thumbed through the tabs. "They did. They just didn't mark the boxes."

She removed the lid of a box on top of the adjacent stack. "After we identify each one, we should put it in order in case we need to find a certain record again. My box has Bs."

"Mine has Ws."

"Great," she said ruefully. "Whoever brought them in just piled them without rhyme or reason."

"At least they're all in one place," he said. "We're lucky they're stored at your house and not where we wouldn't have easy access."

"You're right. I just hadn't realized how many there were."

"You never looked in the basement?"

She shrugged. "I did, but since I had plenty of room for my stuff upstairs, I never gave these files much thought. I had too many other things on my mind."

He glanced at the only empty corner. "Let's see if we can organize them over in that area. We'll stack them alphabetically."

"Good idea." She handed a black Magic Marker to him. "Go to it."

He examined the tabs, then wrote the beginning letters of the last names on the outside of the carton. After repeating the process several times, he hauled the boxes to the wall and systematically arranged them.

Although he moved each with ease, he noticed how Leslie strained to carry hers. As she bent to pick up another carton, he placed a hand on her shoulder and nudged her aside. The brief contact made his fingertips itch to stroke her skin, and for a split second, he forgot his intentions.

"What's wrong?" she asked, straightening.

A man could lose himself in her dark eyes, he thought, before he mentally shook that idea out of his head. Otherwise, he'd spend the afternoon trying to break her rule.

"You label," he said gruffly. "I'll move."

"I can do it," she insisted.

"Sure you can," he agreed. "But you're not used to heavy lifting."

"I move patients all the time."

"Yes, but you also have three or four people to help. I'd rather not haul you to the chiropractor tomorrow." He could think of other places he'd like to take her, preferably ones with soft surfaces and plenty of privacy.

"I'm stronger than I look."

"Yes, but I'm used to tossing around hay bales and wrestling steers. I won't even work up a sweat." To prove it, he moved two boxes while she watched.

"Showoff," she teased with a smile.

"Just considerate of the doctor's muscles," he returned. "On the other hand, I know a few physical therapy tricks."

"Oh, really."

"I'm a pro at applying liniment. If that doesn't work, I have a hot tub that's begging to be used."

"You? A hot tub? Somehow, I can't see you in one. I expected you to be the sort of man who toughed out his aches and pains."

"I was, but then I got older and wiser." He moved the last box she'd labeled. "When you finish a few more, say so."

"Yes, sir."

"Is there anything I should be looking for?"

"A ledger or a similar type of record book. My father sectioned off one corridor of rooms for his obstetrics patients and those who were too ill to stay at home. He could handle about six or eight cases at a time. In an emergency, he even performed the odd appendectomy."

"He was a surgeon?"

"He trained as one," she explained. "But being the only doctor around, he did a lot of general practice work. Once Reno General started expanding and more doctors moved here, he passed his surgery cases to the younger and more experienced surgeons.''

"Then he had a sort of hospital setting at his clinic.''

"Oh yes. He staffed it with nurses around the clock. By the time West View Hospital came into being, he'd doubled his bed capacity.''

"So he needed some means of tracking those patients who spent the night.''

"Exactly. If I'm wrong, and he didn't document who occupied what bed, then we'll have to read through each woman's chart and look for a hospital admission around the time of your birth.''

Zach eyed the cartons around the room. "Now, there's a scary thought.''

"No kidding.''

The first file in the next box caught his attention. "Here's a Hammerstein. Do you suppose he's related to Oscar?''

"Oscar who?''

"Oscar Hammerstein of Rodgers and Hammerstein. You know, they wrote the music for *Oklahoma* and *State Fair*.'' He sang a few choruses from one of Julie Andrews' songs in *The Sound of Music,* pleased that he still remembered the words.

"You sing like a professional.'' Awe filled her voice.

"I can also dance. Anytime you want to two-step, I'm your man. I've also been known to do the lindy and the jitterbug, but only under duress.''

"I always wanted to learn ballroom dance steps,'' she said dreamily. "A friend taught me how to waltz, but it's been years. I doubt if I remember how.''

He pictured the two of them gliding across the dance

floor at the Cattleman's Club. "Sure you will. All it takes is a great partner, and I'm the best."

She laughed. "Your humility is amazing."

He shrugged. "What can I say? I used to be shy until the speech teacher got hold of me in high school. She wanted the drama club to perform the musical *Oklahoma,* but none of her students could sing."

"So she asked you."

He nodded. "I'd been helping with the artwork on the set, and one night, after nearly everyone had gone, I was singing the title song. Mrs. Moore happened to overhear, and she literally ran around the stage trying to find out who it was."

"And a star was born."

"Actually, no. I told her that I couldn't stand in front of a theater full of people. She talked to my choir teacher, and between the two of them, they badgered me into it. She helped me with my stage fright, and by the time I'd graduated, I'd performed in several musicals."

"Where does the dancing come in?"

"People are always dancing in musicals, and of course, that meant I had to learn the steps. In college, I took ballroom dancing as a PE credit, so I can teach you pretty much whatever you'd like to do."

Conflicting emotions of eagerness and indecision appeared on her face. He knew she wanted to accept his offer but couldn't quite do so. Maybe if he took her to the club one evening, just for dinner, and she saw what she was missing, she'd change her mind.

His motives weren't purely altruistic. Dancing would give him a legitimate excuse to hold her close, and he wouldn't stop asking until she said yes.

"We'll see," she said primly.

Encouraged that she hadn't given an emphatic no, he thought ahead to the weekend. He'd have time to send his suit to the cleaners and shine his dress shoes.

For the next half hour, he planned while he worked, and didn't stop until she rose and stretched. At the sight of her long arms above her head and the fabric of her shirt pulled tautly against her breasts, his mouth became as dry as the Nevada desert.

"It's time for a break," she said.

"Sure." He would have agreed to anything she asked for or said.

She grabbed his hand. "Let's go upstairs."

This had to be a dream. "Upstairs?"

"To the living room, silly. I'd like to put my feet up for a while and sit on something softer than concrete."

"Living room. Right." If he didn't straighten out his thoughts, she'd throw him out on his ear. But as he followed her up the stairs, the curve of her derriere made not thinking about her a near-impossible feat. Luckily, by the time they reached the top, he'd managed to regain control.

Seeing her in full sunlight, he chuckled.

"What's so funny?" she asked.

"You. You're a mess." The crisp, professional doctor looked about twelve years old. There was a black smudge on her forehead and one cheek, her white T-shirt and faded blue jeans bore similar smears, and her curls showed traces of gray.

"You're not exactly ready for a night on the town, either," she commented as she removed two soft drink cans from the refrigerator. "Let's go into the living room."

"Are you sure? I mean, we are filthy."

"It's only dust. My vacuum cleaner works."

He chose the vinyl recliner. Compared with the up-holstered sofa, he would do the least amount of damage to it.

"Speaking of a night on the town, my parents are fixing dinner for the family. Would you like to join us?"

"I don't think so."

He hadn't expected her to agree, but he'd hoped. "They'd love to meet Walter's daughter."

"Some other time."

"My mom's a wonderful cook."

She smiled. "I'm sure she is. I'll keep working on these files. Maybe I'll get lucky and find something important."

"Do you know what's funny?"

"No, what?"

"I know Mom and Dad aren't my parents, but I can't think of them in any other way."

"You shouldn't. They're the ones who nurtured you."

"But when we find my—" He stopped himself from saying *real parents.* "When we find the other couple, what will I call them?"

"They'll have names just as Eleanor and Hamilton do."

"I guess so."

"I wouldn't be staging a reunion yet. There are too many variables. First we have to discover their identities, and then it might turn out they've moved or even died."

He hadn't thought of that possibility. After all, Hamilton had suffered a heart attack and only pulled through because of a doctor's quick thinking. Obituaries of people younger than he was appeared in the newspaper every day.

"You're right." He drained the can and crushed it with his hand. "Thanks for the drink. It hit the spot."

The telephone rang, and she rose to answer. "There's more in the refrigerator," she called over her shoulder. "Help yourself."

He would have, but it felt too good to sit in the chair and relax, noting the changes Leslie had brought to the house he remembered visiting over the years.

He recognized some of Dr. Keller's furniture—the curio cabinet, the end tables and lamps. The rest obviously belonged to Leslie. The room had always seemed somewhat bare, a little like his house looked now. But Leslie had added personal touches—colorful throw pillows to match the blue sofa, several paintings of mountain scenes, a Tiffany lamp and a quilted wall hanging of blue irises and lilies.

Pictures of her husband and son must be in her bedroom, he decided, and he was curious to see what sort of man she'd married.

Pieces of fabric lay in a basket near the sofa, and on top was a section of those same scraps sewed together. Suddenly, he understood her fascination with his grandmother's quilt. Leslie was also a quilter. The realization birthed an idea, but he forgot it as she entered the room and he saw her apologetic expression.

"What's wrong?" he asked.

"There was a fire at one of the hotels. The hospital is implementing their disaster plan and calling in all available personnel. I have to go. I'm sorry."

He rose. "I can't say that I'm not disappointed, but I understand."

"Thanks."

"So when can we work on the files again?"

"Tomorrow? I'm scheduled to cover until six for another physician, but even if we start late, we could get in a few hours. Unfortunately, I have to work this weekend, so that's out."

"For me, too. The boys are coming." As much as he was eager to continue searching, he didn't want to forfeit his time with his sons. Monica didn't like to upset her schedule, and if he didn't bring them to the ranch this weekend, he'd have to wait another two weeks.

"Are you doing anything special?" she asked.

"They like to ride, so we'll take a trip into the foothills and camp overnight."

"Sounds like something boys would like to do." Her face grew serious, and she nibbled on her lower lip as if trying to make a decision. "I've been thinking," she began. "Why don't I give you my house key? If you're free before I am tomorrow, you can come in and get started."

Her suggestion surprised him. Obviously, they'd progressed far enough for her to trust him in such a short time. "You're not afraid I'll steal the family silver?" he joked.

She smiled. "Actually, it's the family stainless steel. Somehow, I think my knives and forks are safe. Give me a minute to find my spare key."

He heard her rummaging through a drawer in the kitchen before she returned and placed the key in his palm.

Zach stared at the thin piece of metal. "Are you sure you want to do this?"

She met his gaze, and he tried to read her expression. "No," she said with a small smile, "but it needs to be done. We won't always be able to work together, and this way, we'll still make steady progress.''

He didn't hold any grand notions that her gesture meant anything personal. He also didn't think that she'd suddenly decided to encourage a relationship between them. Giving him a key was simply a logical way to help him with his quest.

Because she so plainly valued her privacy, Zach didn't doubt that Leslie would prefer to go through her father's records by herself or only allow him to help on rare occasions. Yet she knew how badly he wanted this information, so she'd set aside her personal preferences. In that instant, he saw her as a woman who would do the right thing even when it conflicted with her own wishes.

The realization was humbling.

He closed his fingers around the key. ''Thanks. You won't regret this.''

She simply smiled. The distant wail of a siren reminded him that she needed to be elsewhere. He headed for the door. ''See you.''

''Good night.''

His next thought came as a bolt from the blue. Seeing Leslie a few times a week wasn't nearly enough.

LATE ON A FRIDAY afternoon, ten days later, Leslie stared at the towers of cartons still waiting to be explored. Although she'd made progress since they'd begun their search, and Zach had accomplished a lot during the hours he'd spent here while she was at work, the task ahead still seemed daunting.

''Do you suppose we'll ever get through those boxes?'' Zach asked, echoing her thoughts.

''Eventually.''

He opened another one. "It would be nice to know if we were getting close. Zane, my sisters and I would play this game where one of us would hide something and the others would have to find it. The person who knew had to tell if we were hot or cold, depending on how close we were. I wish someone could do the same for us."

"Don't be so impatient," she advised. "Look at it this way. We have to be getting warm. Half of the boxes are on the other side of the room."

"True." He replaced the lid and marked the cardboard with the letter R.

"How was your weekend with the boys?"

"We had a great time. They want to do it again on their next trip home. Would you like to join us?"

"I'm not from pioneer stock," she said.

"If you're scared of wild animals, I'd protect you."

"I'll bet." She wondered what he'd say if she told him that she was afraid of what a weekend trip would mean to him and to his boys.

"I would," he insisted.

"What about food? Do I have to catch my own?"

"Just your main course. I'll be nice and clean your fish for you."

"I'll pass. Worms and I don't go together. They're too squirmy." She shuddered.

His laugh came from deep within his belly. "You're a doctor and you can't handle a worm?"

"It's illogical, I know, but I can't help it." She pulled another carton off the stack and opened it. "I don't like crickets, either."

"What if I bait your hook? Will you come with us?"

His question faded into the background as she saw the contents of her box. Instead of the usual neat files standing on end, loose papers lay on top. She riffled through the documents, identifying the bound books as a complete listing of patients' names, addresses and insurance information. "We are definitely getting warm."

He abandoned his pile to look over her shoulder. "What did you find?"

"I think this is billing information. We must be close to his business records. Check the next box."

Zach pulled the carton off the stack and knelt beside her as he opened it to reveal more bound documents. "This looks like his accounts receivable."

Excitement began to build inside her, and from the gleam in Zach's eye, he felt the same way. "I'll see what's in the next one."

She pulled the carton off the waist-high stack, eager to discover the secrets hidden within. This time, instead of loose papers and bound books, she found a pile of legal-size black leather-bound ledgers with two dates written on the cover. Something inside her screamed that this was the treasure.

Leslie sat on the dusty floor, folded her legs pretzel-style and reverently opened the top book. The headings on each page listed the information she'd hoped to find.

"Zach, I've found it. The book where they kept track of the people they admitted."

"You did?" Once again, he peered over her shoulder. "Are you sure?"

"It has to be. There are columns for an admission date, the patient's name and other vital information, a diagnosis and discharge date."

He lowered himself beside her. "What's the time span?"

She flipped through to the back of the book and compared it to the notation on the front cover. "This ended twenty years ago when my father closed the clinic. The one we want is probably near the bottom of the box.''

Zach removed the next book and noted the dates before he set it to the side. Once he made his way through the box, he sat back on his heels and stared at her. ''That was the last one. We're missing five years.''

As it registered that the day in question fell during those crucial five years, Leslie was certain the disappointment on his face matched hers. They were so close and yet so far away from their goal. ''There has to be another book, if not two.''

Zach rose and opened the next carton. It was filled with more piles of bound material, including her father's final appointment calendar.

''You don't suppose the ledger we want disappeared, do you?'' he asked. ''If someone knew what had happened, they might have destroyed the evidence.''

''I can't imagine anyone destroying the entire book if ripping out a page would serve the purpose. Don't worry. We'll find it.'' She was determined to succeed, no matter how long it took. What had started out as a favor, a case of academic interest, had suddenly become her mission, as well. ''I will say one thing about my father, though.''

''What?''

''He kept *everything*. Here are tax records going back before I was born.''

''He did have pack-rat tendencies,'' Zach admitted, aware of Leslie's sudden shift in attitude. He knew she'd entered into this project halfheartedly, but with their discovery, he sensed she'd been caught up in the drama, too. Once she realized that she cared about this, she might decide she could care about other things, as well, namely him.

Eager to continue, he abandoned his organized system and began to look for ledgers like the ones they'd already seen. His exhaustion vanished as the prospect of finally getting his answers hung within reach, and he whipped through the cartons as if he faced a looming deadline.

His enthusiasm changed to frustration as the trail of business documents and ledgers disappeared.

"Let's stop a minute and catch our breath," she said, placing a hand on his arm.

He stared at her, willing her to understand. "I can't. We're close. I can feel it."

She smiled. "I want to find them as much as you do, but slow down. If we rush, we could miss something."

Knowing she was right didn't make her suggestion easier to accept. "Okay. I'll stop the whirling dervish routine."

"Good."

He opened the last container in his pile and rummaged through the manila folders. "This one has more tax returns." He was ready to relegate it to another pile when his fingers brushed against a book near the bottom. Immediately, he recognized the distinct feel of leather.

Without a second thought, he overturned the lid and began to stack the tax documents inside it. Sure enough, at the bottom of the box rested two ledgers identical to the others. His heart pounded in his ears.

"I think we're so hot, we're going to burst into flames."

Leslie peered over his shoulder. "Oh, my."

For a long moment, he stared at them, wondering if this was how men felt when they discovered buried treasure. Awe, excitement and reverence.

"Aren't you going to look at them?"

He nodded. "I can't help but think the information in those books could change my entire life."

She knelt beside him. "You knew that before we started. Nothing will change unless you let it."

Once again, Leslie was right. He reached in, pulled the top book out and cradled it in his hands, staring at the date.

It was hard to believe that the start of his life had been reduced to an entry between these covers.

"Open it," she ordered.

He sat on the basement steps and with deliberate movements flipped through the brittle pages until he arrived at the date he wanted. Eleanor Dumas's name jumped out at him, and he pointed it out to Leslie. "Here's my mother's entry."

"Who else was admitted that night?"

"Buford Cross for pneumonia. Elliot Parker for a heart arrhythmia."

"I think we can eliminate those two," she said wryly. "Go on."

"Here's one—no, two possibilities. Damn!"

"What's wrong?"

"The page must have gotten wet because the ink smeared, and I can't read the name. I think it says Marvella Anderson."

Leslie gripped his arm to lean closer. "She couldn't be the one."

"Why not?"

"According to this, she was sixty-two. Not the best age for childbearing."

"What about this one?" He pointed as he read. "Rose Rydic. Too bad I can't make out her problem."

Her fingers dug into his arm. He glanced at Leslie

and saw her face light up with excitement. "I think it says OB. Just like it says on Eleanor's entry."

Zach looked at the smudged scrawl. "Are you sure?"

Her gaze remained fixed on the page. "I think so. Doctors' handwriting is notoriously bad. If you can learn to read it, a smear on normal handwriting is a piece of cake."

"I'll take your word for it." *Rose Rydic.* He memorized the name. Was she the one?

"It says here that she was twenty-two." She paused as she squinted over the page. "Zach."

He heard the warning note in her voice. "Yeah?"

She raised her head, met his gaze, and didn't speak. He saw the worry in her eyes, and he stiffened. "What's wrong?"

"It says here, if I'm reading it right, that..." Her voice grew hoarse.

"That what?" He demanded to know.

"She died the same night."

CHAPTER EIGHT

ZACH FELT as if he'd been trapped on a never-ending roller coaster ride. Their discovery of a name had been the highlight of his week. Learning his potential birth mother had died made him feel as if the floor had dropped out from underneath him.

"She died?" he asked incredulously, hoping he'd misunderstood her.

"'Dec' is written in the discharge date column. I'm guessing it stands for 'deceased.'"

His frustration erupted. He jumped to his feet and ran both hands through his hair. "This is just great. Another dead end."

"Not necessarily," she said slowly. "We don't know what happened to her baby. Her husband would surely have taken the baby—or babies, as the case might be—home."

"How would we find out?"

She glanced at the wall of boxes they'd already catalogued. "We find her chart. I didn't run across any Rs. Did you?"

The dead end had just developed a side trail. "One or two. I'll look." He found the two boxes in question. "Nope. These are names from *Ra* to *Ri.*"

"Then the rest of the Rs are in there."

Zach glanced at the piles still waiting for their attention. Although he'd been intent on finding the ledgers, he vaguely recalled seeing folders with names that began with the letter R. He returned to his former section and began going through them again. "I may have seen another box of them over here," he said.

"Let me help." Ten minutes later, Leslie squealed.

"Did you find hers?"

She nodded, her eyes bright as she pulled one slender folder from the box. "Rydic, Rose E. Would you like to read it?"

"Go ahead. You know all that medical mumbo jumbo and can translate."

"Let's take it upstairs where we can see better," she suggested.

Zach hadn't noticed the lengthening shadows in the room until she'd mentioned it. "Fine by me."

He headed up the stairs and stopped when he saw Leslie rummaging in another carton. "What are you looking for now?"

"I want your mother's file, too," she said before she pulled a thicker one out of its carton. "We'll spread everything out on the dining room table. Don't forget the ledger."

He held it aloft. "I didn't." Upstairs, she opened Rose's file and he asked, "What happened the night of October twenty-third?"

She flipped through the pages. "According to this, she came in with labor pains five minutes apart. And then…" She paused to read.

Zach grew impatient. "Then what?"

"Hang on. I'm trying to read my father's handwriting. Apparently, an hour later, she gave birth to a stillborn boy and died minutes later from a hemorrhage." She raised her head. "As far as I can tell, everything seems straightforward. I'm sorry, Zach."

He was, too. "Does it say what her occupation was or list her husband's name?"

Leslie checked the information sheet. "She listed herself as a casino singer and marked single as her marital status. I don't see any mention of her partner."

Zach felt sorry for the woman who'd died alone as an unwed mother, but he was more determined than ever to hunt down his answers. "All this means is that Mrs. Rydic isn't the woman we're looking for. There has to be someone else. Maybe someone came in the next day."

"While you check that out, I'll go through your mother's file."

Zach returned to the ledger and studied the entries both before and after his mother's. Several men, a young boy, two toddlers and three women ranging from fifty to eighty had occupied beds in the Keller clinic.

"Maybe they admitted someone and didn't record it," he said.

"Not likely. From what I've seen, my father took great care to document everything."

"I'm beginning to think the stork *did* just drop us off," he groused, frustrated by how quickly the wheels of information had ground to a halt. He motioned to his mother's file. "Have you found anything interesting?"

"Yes and no. I'm only scanning her history, but did you know that your mother had a miscarriage and delivered a stillborn girl before you and Zane came along?"

"I knew she'd had problems," he said. "That's why they were so excited when we arrived. Mom and Dad both said that we made up for the babies they lost."

"How interesting." She seemed preoccupied.

"What is?"

"Well, according to her prenatal notes, your mother had a difficult pregnancy. She'd been ordered to bed rest for the last few months."

"Isn't it harder to carry twins than single babies? Monica had to stay off her feet quite a bit toward the end."

"That's not all. The baby's heart rate dropped with her subsequent visits. That's not a good sign."

Zach remembered how the doctor had kept close tabs on the twins' fetal heart rates to watch for signs of distress.

She leaned forward. "I can't find any mention of my father suspecting twins. My obstetrics is a little rusty, but the growth measurements taken during her checkups don't add up to a woman carrying two babies. After reading this, I would have expected your mother's baby to be the one who died."

"Wouldn't Eleanor know that she hadn't delivered twins?"

Leslie shrugged. "According to this, she was heavily sedated. She might not have been aware of what was actually going on." Suddenly, she reached for Rose's record and flipped through the pages. "Here's another coincidence. Rose's blood type matches yours."

"It does?"

"Look for yourself."

He saw the report in black and white, and a cold chill scurried down his spine. "Then it's very possible that Rose Rydic was my mother."

"I would say so."

"Who was on duty?" he asked. "Someone has to know what happened."

Leslie examined the signatures of the nurses who'd documented their observations in both Eleanor's and

Rose's charts. "M. Ramirez and B. Memovich," she read aloud.

"Do you know them?" he asked.

It had been a year since she'd heard Barbara Memovich's name, but it still carried the power to stir her anger. She thought she'd put that behind her, but obviously time hadn't softened her resentment toward this woman.

She forced herself to sound nonchalant. "I've heard Barbara's name before."

"We'll have to find them."

Find my father's mistress? Hardly. In spite of her parents' divorce, her life had turned out well, but if Barbara hadn't interfered, Leslie could have grown up seeing her father every day instead of a few times a year.

"I don't know about Mrs. Ramirez," she said, "but Barbara left town after my father died."

"We need to try."

How could she explain that Barbara was the last person on earth she wanted to locate, much less talk to?

He narrowed his eyes. "You seem rather reluctant."

She'd obviously not hidden her thoughts as well as she'd hoped. In a bid to stall for time, she scooted away from the table and pulled a soft drink from the refrigerator. She drank deeply, as much to quench her thirst as to prepare a nutshell version of the story.

"Barbara Memovich was my father's nurse. They had an affair, and afterward, my parents divorced. Barbara stayed with him until he died, although I have no idea where she moved after the funeral." Nor did Leslie want to know.

"I see. Barbara's a touchy subject."

Touchy? Try explosive. "You could say that."

"What about this Ramirez lady?"

"Never heard of her. I'm sure if we look in the business records, though, we'll discover her first name."

"I'm ready if you are."

She smiled at his single-minded determination. They'd found out more in one week, in one *day,* than she'd ever dreamed possible, and part of her was disappointed that their time together was drawing to a close. She was tempted to suggest they call a halt to the evening, but Zach plainly didn't intend to stop until they found Nurse Ramirez's address, talked to her and got the full scoop of the events of the night of October twenty-third.

If they were on the right track with Rose Rydic, then someone in her father's clinic had knowingly switched those babies. She suspected who. She wanted to know why.

"Back to the dungeon," she quipped.

He hesitated at the doorway. "Do you mind? If you don't want to keep looking, I can do it myself."

"We're in this together," she said. "I have questions of my own that need answers."

Because they'd set aside several boxes with tax information for future reference, it didn't take any effort to find them again. By the time they'd found the employee records, it was nearly ten.

"Maria Ramirez." Zach held the page closer to the light as he read. "Here's her last known address and social security number."

"It's too late to call tonight," Leslie said. "I'll check her out first thing in the morning."

He frowned as he continued to gaze at her file. "It won't be that easy. If I remember correctly, a developer demolished a lot of houses on that particular street for a strip mall.''

''Darn.'' She forced herself to look at Barbara's file. The photo attached to her application showed an attractive woman in her thirties, and Leslie immediately tensed. *You can do this,* she told herself as she read the personnel information.

''This form lists her Reno address, which I know isn't correct.''

''Do you have Internet access?''

''Sorry, but I never subscribed after I moved here.'' He straightened and brushed the dust off his jeans. ''When I get home, I'll run a search on my computer. I may find them.''

Rising, she rubbed at the sore spot in her neck. ''Good luck,'' she said, hoping they found Maria first. Intent on smoothing out the kinks, she didn't notice Zach had moved behind her until she felt his hands kneading her upper spine.

Her arms dropped to her sides. ''That feels good.''

''I'm even better with liniment.'' His fingers traveled upward until he reached the base of her skull.

''Mmm,'' she said as the tension began leaving her body.

''I've been thinking,'' he began. ''We should celebrate.''

Immersed in the pleasure of his ministrations, she only caught one word. ''Celebrate?''

''Yeah. We've come a long way in such a short time. We deserve to reward ourselves.''

''We?'' His use of the plural pronoun suggested that he wouldn't find her plan of soaking the dust out of her pores and stitching on her quilt as attractive as she did. ''A quiet evening at home is all I want.''

He clicked his tongue as he shook his head. "Not special enough."

So he wanted something special. "What did you have in mind?"

"Dancing."

Dancing? Having his arms around her all evening? Could she manage it and still keep her heart intact? She twisted to face him. "I have two left feet."

"Not a problem. If you can count one-two-three, you'll be fine." When she hesitated, he added, "If it will make you feel better, I haven't forgotten your rule."

His assurance was some consolation. Surely, she could enjoy an evening with Zach without getting the proverbial stars in her eyes. "Dancing, it is."

"I'll pick you up at six-thirty."

"So early?"

"Dinner comes first," he said firmly. "You can't dance on an empty stomach."

BY THE NEXT EVENING, food was the last thing on Leslie's mind. She didn't hold any illusions that the two of them would visit the Cattleman's Club unnoticed. Zach had too commanding a presence and was too well known as an eligible bachelor, a *wealthy* eligible bachelor, for his movements not to attract attention.

After the publicity generated by the death of her husband and son and her struggle to find a reason to keep living, she'd purposely stayed out of the limelight. Being seen with Zach could undo her efforts to maintain her privacy, but the lure of an evening with him was too great to let the opportunity slip through her fingers.

What an opportunity it was.

The Cattleman's Club reminded her of a gentleman's

establishment from the turn of the century. Dark paneling and scrolled woodwork lined the walls and doorways, while beautifully hand-carved doors separated the various dining rooms. The thick carpeting and the string quartet playing in the background muffled conversations and clinking glasses.

Leslie felt self-conscious on the way to their table as heads turned in their direction. In his tailored gray suit, Zach looked the successful businessman he was, and she sensed the envy of every woman they passed. Leslie might not be dripping in diamonds like they were, but at least she didn't appear dowdy in her old black cocktail dress. Its simple design hadn't gone out of style, and best of all, it fit her better than it ever had.

Even so, she knew that any of the women would happily trade one of their multicarat diamonds to be in her position.

"If looks could kill, I'd be a dead woman," she told him in an aside.

He glanced around and smiled at the people staring at them. "I disagree. If I leave you alone for a minute, you'll be surrounded by adoring men."

"Don't be ridiculous."

"I know what I'm talking about. You're a knockout in that dress."

An embarrassed flush crawled across her cheekbones. "Thank you," she said, pulling off the matching wrap and draping it over the back of her chair. "You look dashing yourself. I must say, you're quite different from the scruffy fellow who stormed into the ER in search of his sister."

He grinned. "Soap and water does wonders."

"The question is, which one is the real Zach Dumas?"

"I'll let you be the judge."

She'd always pictured him as a cattleman who knew his business backward and forward and who wasn't afraid to work beside his crew doing whatever distasteful chore needed to be done. Now, as he spoke with the maître d', inquired about the wine list and the freshness of the seafood, it soon became obvious that he was equally comfortable in this plush, sophisticated environment.

"Are you ready to order, Mr. Dumas?"

Even the waiter knew his name. Didn't the man ever eat at home?

"Leslie?" Zach asked.

Nothing on the menu sounded good, but then an attack of nerves had tied her stomach into a knot and closed off her throat. It wouldn't matter what she requested. She wouldn't be able to swallow. She'd simply choose the cheapest main course so she wouldn't feel quite as guilty about wasting food.

Unfortunately, prices didn't appear on her menu. She hesitated, trying to decide which dish was the most inexpensive, when Zach took charge.

"We'll have the prime rib with all the trimmings. Is that all right with you, Leslie?"

It wasn't, but it seemed tacky to argue. She closed the menu. "Yes. Thank you."

"And a bottle of your best wine." The name rolled off his lips as if he spoke French on a daily basis. The brand sounded far too expensive for her unsophisticated palate.

"French wine?" she asked.

He shrugged. "We're celebrating, remember?"

"Yes, but—"

"Don't argue. You're supposed to enjoy." The wine

steward returned with the bottle, and Zach gave his approval, then sent him away and began pouring. "Tell me about your husband."

"My husband?" She wasn't prepared to talk about Michael or Brandon.

"Yeah. What did he do for a living?"

"He was a computer programmer." At his raised eyebrow, she added, "For an insurance company."

"Had you been married long?"

"Ever since I finished my residency. We met when I was an intern."

"And your son?"

She forced herself to remain objective as she related the information. "He was a cute baby. Always happy. He'd just gotten his first two teeth." She and Michael had taken turns with him throughout the night because he'd been fussy. The next morning, he'd finally dozed off, exhausted, and two beautiful white lines appeared on his gums. Later, they'd celebrated with a glass of wine before going to bed early. It had been their last night together.

Leslie rubbed the stem of the imported crystal, imagining Brandon's sweet baby scent and the way he nuzzled her neck as he lay on her shoulder. So long ago, and yet only yesterday.

"It must have been tough."

Jolted out of her memories and unwilling to share them, she cleared her throat and raised her goblet. "It was." After taking another sip, she diverted the conversation to a less painful topic. "Did you have any luck with your Internet search?"

"I found two dozen entries for Maria Ramirez across the country and five for Barbara Memovich. It will take a while to check them out."

"Were any in Nevada?"

"A few. Why?"

"I'd start with those first. If that doesn't work, we could contact the state board of nursing. Nurses must be licensed, and the agency should have either their current or a forwarding address. Of course, I'm not sure they can share the information, but it's worth a try."

The string quartet stopped playing, and an eight-piece band took their place. The music changed to a peppy number, and Leslie found her foot swaying to the beat.

"Shall we dance?"

"This sounds a little fast for a beginner," she cautioned. "I don't want to embarrass you, or myself."

"Trust me. You'll do fine." He rose and grabbed her hand. "Come on."

Leslie accompanied him to the hardwood dance floor, feeling out of place. Couples glided around them effortlessly, and she stiffened, certain she'd trip over his feet or, worse yet, her own.

Zach took her into his arms, and the familiar tang of his cologne was reassuring. "Relax," he whispered against her ear as he began swaying in time to the beat. "Feel the music. Let it carry you away."

She was plastered against him, and what she felt wasn't the music. As for letting it carry her away... "It's not the music I'm worried about."

"Don't worry about me, either," he said, guiding her into a step. "I know the rules. I won't take you anywhere you don't want to go. Now, stop thinking and start relaxing."

He swung her around until she had no choice but to cling to him like a vine. As he'd said, once she let the music wash over her, it became all too easy to melt against him so that his movements became hers. The

rough twill of his jacket beneath her arms, the sensation
of his hand anchoring her against him, and his unique
fragrance teasing her senses became etched in her mind
as he swept her across the floor. By the time the tempo
changed, she felt as light-footed as Ginger Rogers.

A waltz later, he broke apart. "Shall we stop for dinner?"

She wasn't hungry, but she wouldn't mind resting for
a bit. "Sure. You weren't kidding when you said you
could dance. You're wonderful."

"I get by. The trick is having a partner who can
follow."

Zach had never thought that watching a woman eat
would be a sensual experience, but Leslie proved him
wrong. As her lips closed over her fork, he wanted to
feel their softness against his and to taste the wine on
her breath.

He raised the bottle to refill her glass, but she refused.
"One serving is my limit," she said. "Otherwise I'll
slide under the table."

He chuckled. "Can't hold your alcohol?"

"Not at all." She picked up her roll, and Zach
watched her fingers gracefully separate the two halves.
She had remarkable hands—gentle, competent and
strong. He could hardly wait for her to finish eating so
they could return to the dance floor and he could hold
her in his arms again.

"You're spoiling me, you know," she said.

"How's that?"

"First Armando's and now this. I usually grab something at the hospital or stop at a fast-food drive-through
on my way home. My taste buds won't settle for cafeteria food anymore."

"Then I'll have to make sure those taste buds stay

happy. Would you like dessert? The pastry chef here makes the lightest eclairs.''

She placed her fork on her plate and dabbed her mouth with her napkin. ''Don't tempt me. As it is, I ate more than I thought I would. I'm going to waddle home.''

''No, you won't,'' he assured her. ''You'll get plenty of exercise before we leave.''

Minutes later, the band struck up a slow number, and wordlessly, he drew her to her feet. Once they started, he couldn't seem to stop. The hours passed, and he took advantage of every opportunity to hold her close. He hadn't realized the time until the band took a break at midnight.

Back at their table, Leslie sank into the chair. ''I don't mean to complain, but my feet are going to sue me for abuse.''

''You should have said something,'' he chided, feeling guilty for not noticing her discomfort.

''I was having too wonderful a time.''

''So was I, but I didn't plan to cripple you.''

She smiled. ''Dancing wasn't the problem. I'm just not used to wearing heels. Next time, I'll wear more comfortable shoes.''

The prospect of having a next time thrilled him more than news of beef prices rising. ''I know the perfect place,'' he said. ''It won't be this fancy, but it'll be so low-key you can go barefoot if you'd like.''

''Sounds like fun.''

Companionable silence filled his Bronco during the ride to her house. If she noticed that he took the proverbial scenic route home, she didn't comment. He couldn't remember when he'd spent a more enjoyable evening and he was reluctant for this one to end. Once she'd relaxed, she'd followed his lead on the dance floor as if they'd spent hours practicing. Naturally, he'd limited himself to the simple steps, but given the opportunity, he'd take her through the more complicated ones.

Leslie had made the evening especially pleasant. His dating experiences since his divorce had been few and far between, and while he'd had a passably good time, none of his dates had filled the empty spot inside him. This woman was in a league by herself.

He wanted to know everything about her, from what she thought to how she felt. He wanted to know her hopes, her dreams and what she was like as a child. It was obvious that she'd loved her husband and would never forget him, but he wanted her to look ahead and not behind. Discussing her loss was clearly painful, but time had a way of healing past hurts, and he intended to be ready and waiting when that moment arrived.

She'd reluctantly accepted his invitation, but after seeing her sparkle like sunlight on water, he'd bet one of his purebred bulls that she was glad she had.

What struck him most about the evening was the smile on her face and the laughter in her eyes. Once she'd gained confidence, she'd danced with a surefooted grace that had captured the attention of other couples. She probably hadn't noticed the admiring male glances cast in her direction, but he had, and he was proud to be her partner.

If he hadn't known her to be the distant, aloof ER doctor, he would have thought the vivacious Leslie Hall on his arm was a different person. She may have channeled all her passion into medicine after the tragedies in her family, but tonight proved that she still retained a spark for enjoying life. He was more than willing to work on diverting some of that warmth and excitement in his direction.

He pulled into her driveway and escorted her to the front door. Saying goodbye and good-night seemed anticlimactic, but he had no choice. Given her mood, he could probably talk her into letting him stay, but when it came time for breakfast, he didn't want to lose the ground he'd gained because of second thoughts.

''Would you like to come in? For coffee?''

He wished she hadn't asked. His willpower was too shaky. ''I'd better not.''

''It's a long drive home,'' she said. ''Will you stay awake?''

No problem there. The ache in his groin, that oh-so-sweet agony, would do the trick. ''It won't be a problem.''

The light in her eyes seemed to dim as she turned to insert her key into the lock. A distinct chill filled the air. ''All right then. Good night.''

Their evening had been too special to end like this. ''Leslie?''

She glanced at him, her hand on the knob.

Acting on impulse, he pulled her close and kissed her until he was about to explode with need. The night breeze cooled his overheated skin, but only one thing would quench the fires burning inside him. He'd reach the point of no return soon if he didn't pull on the reins.

Slowly, reluctantly, he changed his kiss from long and deep to soft and tender brushes of his lips. ''Good night.''

She stared at him, her eyes luminous in the street-light's glow. ''Stay.''

''Would you regret it in the morning?''

Her silence gave him his answer.

He kissed her forehead. "I'm going to ask for a rain check, though. When you're ready, I'll cash it in for the full amount."

He hoped that day wouldn't be too far in the future.

CHAPTER NINE

"I'M LOOKING for a nurse who used to live in the area," Leslie told the West View Hospital personnel director on Monday afternoon after her shift had ended. "Her name is Maria Ramirez. I wondered if she had ever worked here."

"I'll have to check our employment files," Cordelia Gaylord told her. "I can't give out any information, though. Privacy issues, you understand."

Leslie had hoped to talk to one of the clerks and not the lady in the power suit who knew every personnel regulation verbatim. This, however, was the luck of the draw. It was a good thing she'd worn the trappings of her profession—a white lab coat with her name and MD stitched on the breast pocket.

"I'm hoping she can shed light on a medical case. Surely you're not going to stand in the way of patient care?" She raised one eyebrow and used her loftiest doctor voice.

"I've been here for five years and I can assure you that the name doesn't sound familiar."

"Perhaps not," Leslie said politely, "but if you're hesitant to find the information for me, I'll be happy to speak with your superior. I'm sure he'll authorize the search. Of course, he'll probably wonder about the lack of cooperation between our departments, but I'm sure the two of you will sort it out."

Ms. Gaylord pursed her lips and frowned. After several tense seconds in their battle of wills, she rose with a sniff and disappeared into the other room.

Leslie mentally patted herself on the back. The threat of going over Ms. Gaylord's head had been hollow, but it had worked. Locating Maria Ramirez was crucial to Zach's investigation, and if she had to tell a few half-truths to get a lead, she would. If her hunch that Maria had remained in the area after her father closed his clinic didn't pan out, then she'd proceed to plan B and contact the state board of nursing.

Ms. Gaylord returned with a file wearing a smirk on her face. "I don't see how this woman can help you," she began.

"She's here? I mean, Maria Ramirez worked here?" She consulted the scrap of paper in her pocket for Maria's social security number and recited it.

"Yes, she did, but as I was saying, I don't see how this woman can help you with your medical case. Her employment was terminated and—"

Leslie couldn't wait. "Isn't there a forwarding address?"

Ms. Gaylord drew her mouth into a hard line. "The city cemetery."

The cemetery? "She died?"

Ms. Gaylord raised one painted eyebrow. "I don't know of any living people who reside at the cemetery."

"When did she pass away?"

"I suppose it wouldn't hurt to give out the information since the woman is deceased," the director said in a patronizing tone. "Ten years ago."

Leslie's hopes sank. "Thanks for your help," she said before she strode from the room. With Maria Ramirez out of the picture, finding Barbara had become imperative. Although Leslie would rather leave her in obscurity, she couldn't do that to Zach. She'd do her part to bring the two of them together.

If her mental turmoil over her father's nurse wasn't enough to cause her sleepless nights, then Zach was. Ever since he'd left her on her doorstep reeling from his kiss, he'd been on her mind. She'd hoped to put the incident behind her, but even today, he invaded her thoughts more often than she liked. Until she figured out how she felt, or *wanted* to feel, about him, that wouldn't stop.

Thank goodness he possessed more sense than she did. She'd all but begged him to stay, to bring back for a few hours the magic that had left her life. As he'd rightly guessed, once the heat of the moment passed, she would regret her impulsive actions.

While she wanted to make love with him and certainly felt strongly enough about him to do so, it would change everything. For her, intimacy implied trust, and until she knew that he wouldn't turn away from her in disgust, she had to keep her hormones under control. If implying that she wasn't ready for a relationship because she still grieved over her husband would slow things down, then she would let the white lie stand. While most people were sympathetic about physical illnesses and didn't bat an eye about seeing a medical physician, not many were as understanding when the illness involved the mind.

In the meantime, Zach's quest took precedence over her private life.

At home, she found a disreputable-looking truck parked on the street and Zach pacing on the porch, dressed in what she'd come to recognize as his work clothes, which included a red bandanna around his neck and a sweat-stained Stetson on his head. "I thought you'd never get here," he told her as she joined him.

"I was checking out a hunch," she said. "You look rather excited. You must have had better luck than I did."

He beamed. "I found her. I found Barbara."

"Where?" She let him inside and kicked off her shoes.

"In Henderson. How did you come out with Maria?"

"Not as well as you did. She died ten years ago."

"Then let's hope Barbara has our answers. If you can take Friday off, a friend of mine who flies corporate jets has room for a few extra passengers on his next trip to Vegas. Flying will save us a six-hour drive, and I'll rent a car for the side trip to Henderson."

Us? "I'm not sure it's a good idea for me to go with you," she began slowly. "You should visit Barbara alone."

"Why?"

She sighed. "Because I might make her uncomfortable."

His expression became speculative. "You're afraid."

"It's not fear," she corrected. "It's…" Her voice died as the right word escaped her.

"Fear."

Perhaps he was right, but she chose to think otherwise. "My showing up on her doorstep would make the situation more awkward than it already is. She's bound to be defensive when you ask her about that night, and having me there will only make it worse."

"I disagree. If you won't go along, then I won't go."

"But, Zach," she protested, "this is your big opportunity. You can't let it slip through your fingers."

"I want you there. You're Walter's daughter. She may tell you things that she won't tell me."

"I can't believe that you'll forget the whole thing if I don't go with you."

"Believe it."

"But, Zach—" she protested.

"We're in this together."

His reminder didn't help. "We are, but—"

"Don't you have questions to ask her, too?"

God help her, but she did. While she could live the rest of her life not knowing the answers, she couldn't bear the responsibility for keeping Zach in limbo.

Leslie drew a deep breath. "All right. I'll go."

"On Friday?" He stood as if poised for action.

She nodded. "Friday, it is."

"It's my weekend to have the boys, so I'll call Monica and arrange to pick them up while we're in town. She'll be thrilled that she won't have to meet me halfway like she usually does."

Clearly Zach had planned their itinerary in minute detail. "You can't spring me on your children without advance notice," she warned. "Seeing their dad with another woman could cause all sorts of problems."

"Let me worry about the boys," he told her. "Everything will work out."

She wasn't as convinced as he was, but she'd tried to warn him. If he chose not to take her admonition seriously, then he would suffer the consequences. It wasn't her place to make the decision.

"Just be ready by seven a.m. Sharp."

She smiled at his imperious tone. "Will you leave without me if I'm not waiting on the porch?"

He grinned as he pulled her close. "No, but you run the risk of me dragging you to my truck as is. Unless you want to meet Barbara and my sons in your nightie, you'd better be rarin' to go.''

With a threat like that, how could she refuse?

BARBARA MEMOVICH'S house was a small Spanish-style bungalow nestled in a cul-de-sac with three others. Tricycles and bicycles lay in the yards of two of the houses, and a stroller stood near the front step of the third, but at the moment, the neighborhood was peaceful and quiet.

It was a complete contrast to what was going on inside Leslie. She dreaded this meeting and had an upset stomach to prove it. Yet she wasn't so self-absorbed that she didn't recognize Zach's inner turmoil. His hard jawline and tight grip on the steering wheel as they'd approached the Henderson city limits had sent her fears into the background. Other than reading street signs and studying the directions he'd pulled off the Internet, their trip through town had passed in silence. And now here they were, parked in front of Barbara's house.

"How are you doing?" he asked.

"Fine. Except for the butterflies in my stomach."

He snorted. "Butterflies? I've got stampeding cattle."

"We could always turn back," she said, offering him a way out.

Zach shook his head. "We've come this far. The only place to go is forward."

"I know." She drew a deep breath and reminded herself to be objective. She was here in an advisory capacity only. "Shall we?"

He took her hand as they ambled up the sidewalk together. For all his tough-guy facade, he obviously needed to feel her presence as much as she needed to feel his.

The door opened before they could knock. A tall, silver-haired woman greeted them at the door with a smile.

"Ms. Memovich?" Zach asked.

"You must be Zachary."

"Yes, ma'am."

"Please come in. And call me Barbara. There's no need to be formal, is there?"

Leslie didn't know what to expect, but it wasn't this self-assured lady who walked so gracefully into her living room. In her mind, she'd pictured Barbara wearing suggestive clothing and enough makeup to single-handedly support a Mary Kay consultant. Instead, she saw an older woman who dressed sharply in subdued colors and had clear blue eyes and a tanned face that didn't require cosmetics.

"You must be Walter's daughter, Leslie," Barbara said in her lilting voice.

"Yes, I am."

"I'm so sorry about your father's passing," she told her. "He was a wonderful, gentle man, and I'm sure you must miss him, along with everyone else in the community. But," she said in a more brisk tone, "you didn't come to hear my condolences."

"No, we didn't," Leslie said, glancing at Zach.

Barbara settled against the cushions of a Queen Anne chair. "Zachary mentioned that you had some questions about the clinic. I'll try to answer them, but remember, it's been twenty years since Walter closed its doors."

"We understand," Leslie assured her. "We're interested in a delivery. Two deliveries, in fact."

"Oh, dear. Walter must have delivered hundreds of

babies. I can't begin to remember specifics about any of them.''

Zach leaned forward, clearly eager to get to the heart of the matter. ''We have reason to believe that something unusual occurred the night my twin brother and I were born.''

''Unusual? Why?''

''It came to my attention in a roundabout way that my blood type doesn't match my parents'. Perhaps you know Eleanor and Hamilton Dumas?''

The smile on Barbara's face suddenly seemed frozen in place. ''Eleanor and Hamilton? Why, yes. I seem to recall their names. I believe they were close friends of Walter's.''

''Tests indicate that they can't be Zach's biological parents,'' Leslie interjected, carefully reading Barbara's response. ''We're trying to determine what may have happened.''

Barbara waved a blue-veined hand in dismissal. ''Why, that must have been close to forty years ago. As I said, we saw so many newborns.''

Zach exchanged a glance with Leslie. Their silent communication seemed to say the same thing. Reluctance, rather than time, had dimmed Barbara's memory. ''We brought the admission ledger,'' he mentioned. ''I'll get it.'' He started to rise.

''That isn't necessary, young man.''

He sat down. An air of expectancy hung over them as her comment confirmed their suspicions. Barbara hadn't forgotten whatever had occurred.

''Are you a reporter?''

''No, ma'am. I raise cattle. I only want to find my roots.''

She addressed Leslie. "And why are you interested?"

"I never really knew my father, and I'd like to know what sort of man he was," she admitted. "If a mistake was made in his clinic, then it's my duty as his daughter to right the wrong."

Barbara's shoulders slumped. The sophisticated lady became a tired old woman before Leslie's eyes. "There was no mistake," she said softly. "And it can't be undone."

Zach perched on the edge of the sofa, his body tense as if poised for action...or for bad news. "What happened?"

Barbara straightened. "You must promise me that this won't be fodder for a tabloid story. I won't see Walter's memory besmirched."

"We promise," Zach said without glancing in Leslie's direction.

Leslie didn't mind that he spoke for her. He already knew how she felt. He might not care about her father's reputation, but he did care about his parents, and on that basis alone, the information Barbara shared wouldn't leave this room.

Leslie had another concern, as well. Any hint of impropriety could have a devastating effect on her career. Granted, she couldn't be held responsible for her father's deeds, but gossip, once started, took on a life of its own. The public would have a field day knowing that Walter's daughter had been under a psychiatrist's care.

Barbara nodded as if convinced by Zach's assurances. "Walter was a family man through and through," she began. "Although he'd trained as a surgeon, he loved delivering babies. In fact, he wanted to fill a house of his own.''

"He did?" Leslie asked, surprised by the information.

"Oh, my, yes. Dear me, I've forgotten my manners. Would you two like something to drink?"

"No." Zach refused for them. He obviously didn't want to wait another minute to hear this story, and neither did she.

"Now, where was I? Oh, yes. As you may be aware, Zach, your mother suffered through difficult pregnancies. First a miscarriage and then a stillbirth. Losing those babies was as devastating to Walter as it was to Eleanor and her husband because he knew how much they wanted children.''

She paused as if caught up in the memory and didn't continue until Zach coaxed her. "What happened that night?"

Barbara sighed. "Eleanor came to us in the late stages of labor, but Walter didn't hear the fetal heart tones. She was in horrible pain, and he sedated her, not wanting her to suffer while she delivered what he suspected was a stillbirth. We were working with her when another of our OB patients came in, only minutes away from delivering.''

Zach supplied the name. "Rose Rydic."

"How did you know?" Barbara asked, clearly surprised.

"We found the admission ledger," Leslie answered.

"Oh. Yes, well, Rose was such a pretty woman. We couldn't understand why she wouldn't consider adoption if she wouldn't marry her baby's father. Girls in her situation usually did one or the other." She shook her head. "Even after we suspected she was carrying twins, she wouldn't budge. Lord only knows how she would have supported one baby, much less two, as a singer.''

Leslie squeezed Zach's hand. Knowing that Rose had wanted to keep her babies surely gave him some consolation. ''So Rose came to the clinic. Then what?'' she asked.

''I put her in the room next to Eleanor's. There were two of us on duty that night, so I sent Maria to stay with Eleanor while I helped Walter with Rose. Ten minutes later, she delivered a baby. Fifteen minutes after that, a second little boy arrived.''

She glanced at Zach. ''Those little fellows were as beautiful as their mama and as healthy as could be.''

Touched by the comment, Leslie glanced at Zach for his reaction. He sat stone-faced and tense. ''Did she know about us?'' he asked.

Barbara's eyes glistened with tears. ''Yes. After we told her about her two sons, she was so proud.'' Her voice choked. ''The smile on her face was absolutely breathtaking.''

''Did she say anything?'' His voice sounded hoarse, indicating that he wasn't as unmoved as he tried to appear.

Barbara nodded. ''She told us to be sure and take good care of her boys.'' She dabbed at her eyes. ''Of course we did.''

''When did she run into problems?'' Leslie asked, threading her fingers through Zach's to lend moral support.

''While I was cleaning up the babies and getting them ready for Rose to hold, she started fading fast. Walter finally controlled the bleeding, but shortly after, Rose's heart just stopped. He tried CPR, but it was no use.''

Leslie had seen plenty of deliveries in her obstetrics rotation and could easily imagine the scene—a tired, worn-out mother summoning enough energy to ask about her children. Then, after learning they were healthy and perfect, drifting off to sleep, expecting to see them when she awoke.

In Rose's case, she didn't wake up.

"Meanwhile," Leslie coaxed, "what was happening with Eleanor?"

Barbara pinched the bridge of her nose. "While your father was finishing with Rose, Maria came running in to tell us that Eleanor's baby was crowning. Walter left the babies to me and went to help Eleanor. I listened for a baby's cry but I never heard one. I knew it wasn't a good sign.

"As soon as I had settled the twins, I went over to help. While he worked with her, I saw the baby lying in the bassinet, and I knew." She shook her head. "Eleanor never realized."

A pang of sorrow pierced Leslie's heart. She'd lost one child and had been devastated to the point where she couldn't function. It had taken drastic intervention to pull her from the brink of despair into the land of the living. She couldn't imagine losing two, or even three.

"Back in those days, the men stayed in the waiting room, so Hamilton never knew, either. Oh, I have a feeling that he sensed things weren't right when he brought her to us. He was so worried about her and the baby.

"As soon as she was resting, Walter turned to me with tears in his eyes. He knew Eleanor couldn't emotionally survive another stillborn baby and he hated having to tell her. He aged ten years that night."

"When did you decide to switch us?" Zach asked.

"I'm getting to that. Just then, one of the twins started crying. Walter heard him, and suddenly, his eyes brightened, and his grim expression disappeared. He picked up Eleanor's baby and left the room. He had something in mind, I could see it by the determination on his face, but I didn't realize what he was doing until I saw him place the dead baby in Rose's arms."

She slowly shook her head. "I'll never forget what he told me when I asked him what he was doing. 'Barbara,' he said. 'We lost two lives tonight. I can either tell the truth and destroy four more, or take matters in my own hands.'"

As she considered the path her father's thoughts had taken, Leslie could see that the moral dilemma must have weighed heavily on both of them. Without Barbara's complicity, her father's good deed would have backfired. This was a startling new side to her image of Walter Keller. If he could risk his career for his friends' emotional well-being, then he couldn't have been the coldhearted workaholic her mother had described. How distressing to realize she'd seen only what her mother had wanted her to see.

"What did you do?" Leslie asked, her voice shaky.

"I still hadn't caught on until he reminded me that Rose didn't have a husband and, as far as we knew, no family. Her babies would go to a foundling home while his friends would go to their ranch with empty arms. When he looked down on the twins—one of you was sucking your thumb at the time—I suddenly understood. Here was a couple wanting a baby, and two babies needing parents. It seemed a match made in heaven."

"So he made the switch," Zach said.

"Actually, I did. I moved the two of you into

Eleanor's room, and as soon as everything was in order, he brought in Hamilton.'' Her smile was gentle, and her eyes once again took on a far-off gleam as if she were witnessing the event. "I felt so guilty, but I honestly thought Hamilton would burst his buttons when he came in and saw the three of you fast asleep. It was such a touching sight.''

Zach leaned back against the cushions, as if overwhelmed by the story. Leslie certainly was.

"I'll be honest," Barbara continued. "The deception bothered me, but only until the next morning when I gave you to Eleanor to hold for the first time. I declare, her smile was as bright as the sun, and in my heart, I felt at peace. And when she talked about planting a rosebush in each of your honor, I knew we'd made the right decision.'' She shrugged. "I never heard of anyone doing that before, and I'd like to think it was a sign that we had Rose's blessing.''

Leslie remembered the rosebushes lining Zach's porch. It was early in the season, but they'd appeared hardy and healthy, as if they'd been well-tended. Now she understood why.

"Whenever Dr. Keller visited my folks, he always asked us how we were doing,'' Zach mentioned in an offhand tone. "Even if he only stayed long enough for a cup of coffee, he wouldn't leave until he'd said hello. We felt so important because someone as busy as he was had taken time for us.''

"He kept close tabs on you," Barbara admitted, "but he never had any doubts about the love you'd receive. Your parents doted on you both. I could see it when they brought you to the clinic for your checkups.

"Walter had taken something tragic and turned it into something wonderful and precious. I'll bet you never knew that whenever he lost a patient or felt like a failure, he'd visit you. He always came back refreshed.''

"I didn't know. I wonder if my parents ever noticed the connection, either.''

"He considered your family his greatest success story. As he watched you grow into fine young men, he never regretted his decision. Neither did I.''

Leslie felt, then saw Barbara's attention fix upon her. She sat rigidly, waiting for the retired nurse to share what was obviously on her mind.

"As for you, dear girl,'' she finally said, "your father loved you more than anything. He wanted you to have brothers and sisters, but after you were born, your mother moved into another bedroom. Your father turned to me.''

Leslie listened in surprise. Her mother had never shared that part of the story with her. "I didn't know.''

Barbara smiled. "I'm not surprised. After working with him, I'd grown to love him, and if your mother didn't want him, then it was her loss. Walter wanted to marry me, but I felt guilty over breaking up his marriage, so I couldn't. I wanted to, though. I suppose I didn't think I deserved to be completely happy at your expense. We stayed together for years, and I don't regret a single moment. I've missed him every day since he died.''

Leslie's throat clogged with emotion. "So have I,'' she said. So many had suffered. If her mother were still alive, she'd confront her, but she wasn't. Barbara's statements rang true, though. Leslie's mother had never been demonstrative, doling out hugs and kisses with her cookies and milk. The last time Leslie had been tucked in was before her father moved out, and he had been the one to read her a bedtime story. To think she'd completely blamed her father for the divorce when it wasn't the case.

I'm sorry, Dad.

She rose stiffly. The afternoon had been profitable, but emotionally draining. She wanted time alone to sort through her tangled thoughts. "Thanks for talking to us," she told Barbara. "We appreciate it."

Zach echoed her thanks as Barbara led them to the door. "I'm glad I was able to answer your questions," the older woman said simply. "Right or wrong, Walter had his patients' best interests at heart. Please don't judge him too harshly."

Leslie nodded. "Thank you again."

Zach stopped in the doorway. "What happened to her? To Rose's body?"

"We notified the woman who ran the boardinghouse where she lived. As far as I know, her landlady took care of the funeral arrangements."

"Do you remember her name?"

"I'm sorry. It's been too long, and I never met her. I'd heard a rumor that Rose worked for her landlady's brother in his casino, but I don't know that for a fact."

"Do you know which one?" Zach pressed.

Barbara slowly shook her head.

"And she didn't give you any clues about our father?"

"I wish I could tell you," Barbara said gently, "but she never said a word about him, who he was or where he lived. I don't even know where *she* came from."

Leslie took Zach's arm. "That's all right. You've been more than helpful."

Zach silently walked beside her to their rental car. Leslie sensed that Barbara's explanation had affected him more than he cared to admit. "Are you okay?" she asked.

"As well as I can be, considering my whole life has been a lie. Not just mine, but my parents', as well."

"If it was a lie, it was a very pleasant lie. For all you know, you had more advantages than you would have had otherwise."

"Maybe."

During the short return trip to Las Vegas, they talked of inconsequential things, as if they couldn't discuss the subject uppermost on their minds until they'd each taken time to fully assimilate the information. To her relief, Zach's pensive mood lightened as they approached his ex-wife's house. It disappeared completely when Keith and Kenny barreled out of the house, shouting war whoops as they grabbed Zach around the waist.

A tendril of envy twisted around Leslie's heart. Being near infants and toddlers was tough, but the twins were so much older than her son that sharing their company was easier.

"This is Leslie Hall," he told his two boys, who seemed more interested in their upcoming weekend than in her. They were carbon copies of their father, and even if she hadn't known they were Zach's sons, she would have suspected it once she saw them together. She wondered if Zach and Zane bore as strong a resemblance to their father, whoever he might be, as these two did.

Keith and Kenny wore impish grins on their freckled faces. Fortunately for her, Keith wore a striped T-shirt while Kenny wore one in solid blue. She'd be able to tell them apart on the way home.

"She's a doctor," Zach added.

Keith stared at his father. "Are you sick?"

"No."

"Then how come you brought a doctor along?" Kenny asked.

"Because I wanted company on the way here. And I wanted Leslie to meet you."

"Oh. Are you going camping with us?" Kenny asked her.

Leslie smiled. "I'm afraid not."

"Maybe next time," Zach added.

"Cool," Keith said. "If Kenny gets a fishhook stuck in his hand again, we'll have a doctor to yank it out instead of Dad."

Zach leaned close to speak in her ear. "And you thought they wouldn't want you around."

"Wait until I make them wash their hands before we eat," she warned with a smile. "They'll change their tune."

Throughout their relatively short flight to Reno, the boys regaled them with tales of school and plans for the upcoming weekend. Before long, they'd transferred the boys' gear from the plane to Zach's Bronco and were on their way to Leslie's house. She intended to give everyone a platonic goodbye before she stepped onto the curb, but Zach insisted on walking her to her door after admonishing the boys to stay put.

"I hate to leave you alone," he said.

"Why?"

He shrugged. "It's been a tough day."

"For you, too." The horn honked, and as she glanced in the Bronco's direction, two boys wearing wide smiles waved. "You've been paged."

"I'll take the boys home Sunday afternoon. Can I stop by on the way back?"

She grinned as she once again glanced in the twins' direction. "Will you have the energy?"

"For you? Always."

CHAPTER TEN

ZACH BOUNDED up Leslie's porch stairs two at a time. As late as it was and as tired as he felt, he should have driven straight to his ranch after delivering Keith and Kenny back to their mom, but he simply couldn't. He needed to see Leslie and he couldn't wait another twenty-four hours.

As he raised his hand to poke the doorbell, the door swung wide. Light spilled onto the porch, and he could see Leslie's welcoming smile.

It made him feel as if he'd come home. His nerves had been as taut as a newly strung wire fence all weekend, but now his tension eased. Leslie Keller Hall was more powerful than a tranquilizer.

"Hi," he said, suddenly feeling like a gawky teenager picking up his first date.

"Zach," she exclaimed as she let him inside. "I was beginning to think you'd changed your mind and weren't coming."

His awkwardness passed as her calming influence brushed over him. "We were running late. Kenny left his shoes and we had to backtrack so he could have them for school tomorrow. I was afraid you'd gone to bed."

"At nine o'clock?" she scoffed. "Hardly. I don't need much sleep."

"I'm sorry I didn't get here earlier. I'd planned to take you to the ranch."

She raised one eyebrow. "Didn't you drive enough miles today?"

"I wanted to show you the sunset."

"I saw it from my front porch," she said.

"Yeah, but I have this outlook on the northwestern ridge of my property. There isn't a better view in the entire county," he boasted.

She grinned. "Is that supposed to entice me to join you?"

"Yeah. Is it working?" he asked hopefully.

"I'll let you know. Is this the Dumas equivalent to Lover's Lane?"

He grinned. "More or less."

"Your father allowed you to take your dates there?" She tsked. "I'm shocked."

"Actually, the location was a well-kept family secret. Dad didn't let us in on it until Zane and I were both married."

"Smart man. I imagine he had his hands full with the two of you without adding your hormones to his list of worries."

Zach grinned. "Zane was the evil twin. I was the good one."

"A likely story."

Satisfied that he'd planted the idea of sharing a sunset in her head, he let the subject drop so the seed would sprout and take root. He sniffed the air, noticing it smelled different from the scented candles she usually burned. This aroma was good enough to eat, reminding him that the sandwich he'd grabbed several hours earlier no longer stuck to his ribs.

"Something smells delicious."

"Brownies and hot apple cider. Want some?"

"Need you ask?"

"I didn't think so."

He followed her into the kitchen and watched her place two mugs of cider in the microwave and set the timer. "That's what I miss most at my place. The smell of something baking."

"Your wife cooked a lot?"

"For all of Monica's faults, she always had cookies, a cake or a pie ready to eat. After trying out her recipes on me, I guess that's why she started her own catering service in Vegas."

She placed a brownie on a napkin. "What about your mother?"

"She baked a lot, too. All of the Dumas men have sweet tooths, in case you didn't know it. She would throw in a loaf of homemade bread for good measure. There's nothing like a piece of fresh bread, hot out of the oven, slathered with butter. Just thinking about it makes me drool."

He held out his hand for the brownie, but she slid it out of reach. "If your taste buds are set for homemade bread, I'll just save this—"

"Oh, no. A brownie will fill my hollow spot just fine."

He pressed her against the countertop so he could lean past her and snag it, but the playful moment swiftly became intimate. Her vanilla scent, the smell of chocolate surrounding her and the feel of her body against his were enough to take his mind off his stomach and focus on other body parts. Hers in particular.

He moved away reluctantly. "You cheated," he said softly.

"How?"

"You've already eaten a piece," he accused, aware of the chocolate on her breath.

"I licked the bowl," she corrected. "I couldn't eat one."

"Why not?"

"Because if you didn't come, I was going to take these to work in the morning. I've never brought treats, so I thought I'd take a turn."

He wondered if she realized that such a small gesture was a first step toward opening herself to her co-workers. "You'll have to make another batch, because by the time I'm through, you won't even have crumbs left."

She smiled. "Promises, promises." As she spoke, she slid the napkin toward him.

He bit into the square. "Mmm. Delicious. Family recipe?"

"Betty Crocker," she answered as she placed a steaming mug of cider in front of him. "And since it's from a box, you don't have to ooh and ah over it."

"Yes, I do." He finished the one in three bites and held out his hand for another.

"You look tired."

"I am," he admitted, although he'd gotten his second wind as soon as he'd entered her house. "After sitting in the car, I'd rather stand, if you don't mind."

"Not at all. Did the boys wear you to a frazzle?"

He shook his head. "I didn't sleep very well the last two nights. I couldn't stop thinking about everything."

She leaned against the counter and folded her arms in a relaxed pose. "For instance?"

Zach forced his attention off her long legs. Where should he begin? "I could see my dad bringing my mother to the clinic, worrying about her and the baby

and pacing a path in the waiting room. Whenever anything bothered—*bothers* him—he never can sit still. After being in the delivery room with Monica for the boys'
birth, I always felt sorry for Dad. Not knowing what's
happening can play tricks on your mind because you
tend to think the worst.''

''Like with you and Melinda.''

Zach grinned, remembering how he'd worn a path in
the floor during his sister's stint in the hospital. Maybe
he was more like Hamilton than he thought. ''He had
to be worried about losing the baby, or my mother, or
both. Especially after he'd gone through this twice before….'' He couldn't finish.

''I'm sure he had faith in Walter.''

''Yeah. Anyway, watching my boys hammered home
how difficult it must have been for Eleanor to lose two
children. My parents never really talked about it, and
when they did, they glossed over the details. After hearing Barbara's account, I put myself in their shoes. I kept
thinking of what I'd do if I lost my sons. It was too
painful to imagine.'' He paused. ''I guess your career
helped you cope.''

Although he'd hoped she would share her experience,
Zach sensed her slight withdrawal. ''Eventually, yes, it
did,'' she answered. ''Tell me about the rosebushes.''

Once again, he noticed how she diverted the conversation in another direction. ''According to Dad, Mom
planted two yellow bushes for the two babies she lost,
red for Zane and me, and pink for Melinda. When Kerry
came to live with us, Mom planted another pink variety
for her so she wouldn't feel left out. We had our little
ceremony the day the adoption was finalized.''

''How sweet. What a wonderful tradition.''

''It is, and Mom still oversees the care of *her* roses.''

He grinned. "Once I bought a different brand of fertilizer than she usually used, and she insisted I return it and get the right one. I phoned every greenhouse in the county before I found what she wanted, but I did, and she was happy."

"I'll bet you never made that mistake again."

"Nope."

"How *do* you feel about what Barbara told us?"

He thought back to the moment when the retired nurse confirmed his suspicions. "At first I was numb. In shock, I suppose. It's one thing to speculate on the truth and another to hear it confirmed."

"Whoever coined the phrase, 'the truth sometimes hurts,' knew what they were talking about," she said kindly.

"I thought I'd be able to listen to her story objectively, as if the facts pertained to someone else, but during odd moments with my boys, I went over the things Barbara said. Everything I'd heard became *my* story, *my* history and my boys' history."

The now-familiar rush of conflicting emotions ran through him again before one seemed to predominate.

"How do you feel now?"

"I'm not in shock anymore," he said. "Right now, I'm angry." After two days, his anger had driven him to seek her out, in spite of the late hour and his physical exhaustion. If anyone could help him regain his perspective, it would be Leslie.

"It's a typical reaction," she said. "First shock, then anger, and then finally adjustment."

"Well, right now I'm stuck on step two. Your father and his nurse had no right to make that decision."

"Probably not," she agreed. "As physicians, we're trained to save lives. But I understand why my father was worried about your mother's mental well-being and why he wanted to spare her further anguish when he had the means to do so.''

"He still should have told her the truth," he insisted. "Friends don't lie to each other."

His comment reverberated through her like the toll of a bell. While she'd never told him a direct falsehood, a lie of omission was still a lie. Would he be as upset with her when he learned how far her despair had driven her?

Leslie squared her shoulders. "Even if it would spare them pain?"

He shook his head. "Zane and I deserved to know the circumstances surrounding our birth. The ends don't justify the means."

"I'm sorry you feel that way," she said stiffly. "Not everything is black and white. There are shades of gray."

"There shouldn't be."

"There are," she said, thinking of the murky areas in her life. "I'm not condoning my father's actions, but I do applaud him. He did a very brave thing."

"Brave? Since when is not telling the truth an act of bravery? It would have been more honorable to be honest."

"And where would honesty have gotten you?" she demanded. "With a set of foster parents? Or with people who couldn't give you what Eleanor and Hamilton did?"

"Dr. Keller should have explained, even if he didn't share the story with anyone else. They would have kept the secret."

Zach simply wouldn't let go of his anger, but Leslie

was equally determined to defend her father. It was the least she could do for him.

"Perhaps," she admitted. "But how many people can know a secret before it's no longer considered one? Do you realize what would have happened if the truth ever came out? He could have lost his license, not to mention what would have happened to you and your brother. You both would have been whisked off to a foster home faster than you could have packed your bags or said goodbye. Do you think it would have been easier on Eleanor and Hamilton to raise you with the fear that a slip of the tongue would bring someone to take you away?

"Suppose your parents knew about Rose and they entrusted this secret to you. Could you and Zane have kept it? And would that knowledge have made any difference in the way you loved the Dumas family?"

He fell silent. "I just feel as if we've lost so much of our history."

She drew a calming breath. "From what Barbara said, Rose didn't mention any family or friends. You wouldn't have known any more than you do now."

"Hamilton could have hired private investigators."

"And risk losing the boys he was raising as his own? I doubt it. At least this way, you can't hold anything against your parents, because they didn't know any more than you did.

"As for your history," she said gently, "you have the name of your birth mother, Rose Rydic, and Barbara filled in the details she could. Whether you continue searching or not, the important thing is that Rose gave you life and the Dumases nourished it. Isn't that the best history anyone could have?"

He rubbed his face with his hands, and Leslie saw

the exhausted slump to his shoulders. Clearly, he'd lost some of his fight. "You're right," he said slowly. "But I still want to know where she came from and who my birth father was."

"Then keep looking. Just don't be disappointed if it takes years to find your answers."

"I know. I wonder how I'm going to tell my parents about this."

"That's a decision you and Zane should make together."

"I don't know where he is or when he'll be back. I'd rather not wait indefinitely."

"You've waited thirty-eight years. Another few days or weeks won't matter," she advised him. "You're tired, so don't decide anything today."

He smiled. "The voice of reason. Thanks."

She touched his arm. "Are you feeling better now?"

"Yeah."

The urge to comfort him grew stronger than her ability to keep a friendly distance. She reached out and hugged him. "I'm glad."

He flinched, and she let go. "What's wrong?" she asked.

"Sorry about that," he apologized. "You just pressed on a sore spot."

"Where?"

"On my back. It's no big deal."

Her clinical training surfaced at his mention of a sore spot. For him to react so strongly, the area obviously pained him more than he wanted to admit. Considering the size of the bulls he worked with and their volatile tempers if a mere human got in their way, she envisioned something serious. "What happened?"

"It's embarrassing, really," he began.

"Doctors are immune to embarrassing stories."

"Yeah, well, Keith and I had a little accident with his fishing pole."

She tried to think of an injury with a fishing pole that would result in a hurt back and came up blank. "You'll have to be a little more specific."

"Keith's always had trouble casting so I was teaching him what to do. He thought he had the hang of it and wanted to do it by himself. I stood back and he let it fly. Unfortunately," he said wryly, "he pressed the button too soon, and when he drew his arm back, the line released and the hook caught me on my back. When he threw his arm forward, he tried to take me with it."

She winced, imagining the pain of the steel barb. "Oh, dear. Well, off with the shirt so I can see the damage."

"It's only a scratch," he said as he unsnapped the front closures.

"How do you know?" she asked. "Do you have eyes in the back of your head?"

"No, but Kenny said it was only a scratch."

"You're trusting your health to a ten-year-old?"

Zach shrugged. "I didn't have much choice. Keith was too shook up to be of any help. It really didn't hurt, so I figured there was more damage to my shirt than to me."

"I'll be the judge of that. Did you disinfect it?"

"Kenny doused it with alcohol. Stung like the dickens, so it must be okay."

She shook her head. "Men," she said in mock disgust. As his shirt came off, exposing miles of chest and acres of skin, her frustration over the male species in general turned to admiration of one man in particular.

Her fingers itched with the desire to feel the texture of the light smattering of hair on his chest.

Get a grip, she scolded herself. *You're a doctor, and at the moment, he's a patient.* "Turn around," she said, hiding her reaction to his sculpted form behind a brusque tone.

He obeyed. "Be gentle with me," he joked.

Lord! The sight of his broad shoulders was enough to melt her into a puddle. She forced herself to be objective, as if he were any other male who'd strolled into the ER needing attention. She studied what he'd described as a scratch and frowned at what she saw.

"You guys really do need a doctor with you when you're camping."

"Then you'll join us next time?"

"Maybe. Do you want the good news or the bad news first?" she asked.

"Give it to me straight. I can take it."

She drew a breath. "Your so-called scratch is about eight inches long and is a lot deeper than what I'd consider a scratch. It's also red and oozing, which tells me there's an infection brewing. Fishhooks aren't exactly sterile."

"And the good news?"

"You don't need stitches. With proper care, it shouldn't get worse."

"That is good news. Do you know where I can find a doctor to work such a medical miracle?"

"I can recommend one," she said dryly. "Come on. Off to the dining room. I'll be right in as soon as I get my medical bag."

She returned, carrying a box with a big red cross on the lid and a large bottle of peroxide. He eyed the bottle and the supplies she laid out. "That stuff doesn't burn, does it?" he asked.

"I haven't heard any complaints. If it does, I'll blow on it."

"Promise?"

"Promise."

She began to clean the injury, paying careful attention to the weeping areas. Probing the wound must hurt, but he was acting like a typical male, enduring pain stoically. She wondered if he did it all the time, or just for her benefit.

"How are you doing?" she asked when she saw his fingers clenched into a white-knuckled fist.

"Okay." His curt response and the underlying roughness in his voice suggested that her ministrations weren't as painless as she would have liked. "I'll live."

"I certainly hope so," she teased. "It wouldn't do much for my reputation, otherwise."

After she cleaned his injury to her satisfaction and smeared on antibiotic cream, she taped a long strip of gauze over the area. "To keep you from rubbing the cream onto your shirt," she said.

"I could go without one."

"You could," she agreed. "It might raise a few women's eyebrows as you drive home, though."

"Since I'm not planning on leaving yet, I guess it doesn't matter."

Her pulse began to race. It was getting late, but fool that she was, she didn't want him to go. The weekend had passed in slow motion, but once he'd walked through her front door, time had flown by. "Oh?"

He grabbed her around her waist and pulled her close, his touch sending delicious shivers down her spine. "I need to find out how I can pay the lady doctor."

She smiled at him. "My rates are extremely high."

"How high?"

"How much can you afford?"

"For you, darlin', the sky's the limit," he drawled as he pulled her onto his lap.

"In that case, I'll have to think of the proper form of payment," she said, conscious of how close his mouth hovered and how strong his arms felt around her. "Including an amount that's appropriate for the services rendered."

"Well, if we're thinking of exchanging services," he began, "maybe I could take a turn at playing doctor?"

She grinned at his hopeful expression. "I don't have any wounds," she told him.

His hand moved to the area of her heart. "I think you do."

She froze. The lighthearted moment had become far more serious. "And you think you can fix them?"

"I think so, yes. I'd sure like to try."

He couldn't repair what he didn't know was wrong, but telling him about those days when she'd wanted to die and had tried her best to achieve that end took more courage than she possessed.

"How do you intend to do that?" she asked instead.

His grin was the same lazy smile she'd seen many times before. "First, I'd start with this." Immediately, he bent his head and pressed his mouth to hers.

The kiss Leslie had experienced before suddenly seemed mild compared with this one. She hardly felt his hand under her chin, raising her head enough to grant him easier access to her lips. His touch was full of passion and of promise, at the same time reminding her of how empty her life had been until he'd stormed in and of how needy she'd continue to be if she didn't let him fill those holes inside her soul.

Logic demanded that she stop before things went too far, but his mouth worked a magic that sent good sense sailing out the window. For the first time since the death of her husband and son, she felt a strong emotion other than grief stirring inside her. It had been so long since she'd desired a man, and the idea of calling a halt was suddenly not an option.

His mouth moved, and she heard him speak as if from a distance. "And then..." He nibbled on her lower lip as his hand slipped underneath her shirt and cupped her breast. "Actually, I'm more of a show rather than tell kind of guy."

"Then show me," she begged.

"I will," he promised as he continued his onslaught.

Clothing seemed extraneous and before she realized it, he'd pulled her T-shirt over her head and was fumbling at the clasp of her lacy bra.

"My, my, darlin'," he mumbled against her earlobe. "It's a good thing I didn't know what you were wearing under your clothes or I wouldn't have held out this long."

The hook gave way, and she leaned into his hands, eager for his touch. She should have been cold, but heat roared through her veins until even her shorts seemed too confining.

Before she could slide them off, he stood, carrying her as if she weighed no more than a child. "Where's your bedroom?"

"Down the hall. Second door on the right."

He strode in that direction and set her on the edge of her bed. The short delay restored part of her good sense, and she clambered to her feet before he could follow her onto the mattress. "Maybe we need to slow down for a minute."

"Slow down? Honey, I don't think that's possible."

She held a hand on his chest in a feeble attempt to force him to stop and listen. "Don't get me wrong. I want this more than anything."

"But?" His eyes were dark pools in the dimly lit room.

"But there are things you don't know about me."

"Now, darlin', that's exactly what I'm trying to do—to learn everything about you, from head to toe."

She felt ridiculous, trying to hold a serious discussion while both of them were half-clothed. "Zach, you need to listen...."

"I am, but you're not saying anything. There are things I don't know about you, and vice versa. We'll find out everything we need to know about each other in due time."

"But, Zach."

"Were you in prison?" he asked.

Only in one of my own making. "No," she began.

"Then whatever it is isn't that important," he said as he tugged her bra straps over her shoulders and tossed the scrap of fabric onto the floor. "What's done is done. Look to the future."

He made it sound so simple, and she said so.

"It is simple," he said, pulling her close. "Enjoy what we have at this moment and in the moments ahead. Nothing else matters."

Heaven help her, but she believed him. She didn't want to delay another second. Someday she'd tell him the truth, but for now, she'd give herself to him, and in the process let him heal the wounded places in her soul.

He lowered his mouth to her collarbone. "Now, if

you don't mind, you're interfering with my prescription.''

"We can't have that, now, can we?'' she said, breathless.

His hands stroked every inch of her exposed skin while she ran her fingers over him, careful of his bandage. He was patient and tender, handling her as if she were made of spun glass.

She trembled, hardly able to stand on her feet for all the explosions going off inside her. She fumbled at the waistband of his jeans, working on the zipper, which seemed to catch instead of glide easily. He stopped to help her, and at last, he stepped out of his jeans.

Her shorts went next, slithering down her legs until skin met skin. His fingers traveled down her abdomen, and when they stopped at the entrance of her silken softness, she shivered with anticipation.

"Cold?" he asked.

"No," she breathed.

He pulled away again, but before she could complain about his momentary absence, he returned with the foil packet he'd retrieved from his jeans pocket. Seconds later, she felt herself being lowered onto the soft sheets before his hard, lean frame completely covered hers.

Once again, his motions were slow, deliberate and clearly calculated to drive her crazy. She didn't want to wait, but he drove her to the edge, then pulled her back as if preparing her to take the final step.

She wanted this. She craved it. Everything he did seemed focused on her needs, her wants, her desires, and she tried to return the favor. She stroked his heated skin, marveling at the strength of him, but he stopped her.

"I don't want this to end too soon," he said.

"But—" she protested weakly.

"Don't argue," he murmured as he moved to lavish equal attention on her breasts. All she wanted was for him to ease the ache he'd created, quench the flames he'd ignited....

She wanted to beg, she wanted him to finish his tender torment, when at last he finally slid into her and began a gentle rhythm that gradually accelerated until she felt as if she'd exploded into a million pieces.

Slowly, she returned to the present, feeling the whisper of his breath against her neck and the steady thump of his heartbeat against her hand. His scent mingled with the fragrance of her room in a heady combination.

Zach carefully rolled off her and tucked her under his arm.

"This could become addictive," he warned.

"Could?" she asked. As far as she was concerned, it was fact, not possibility.

"Sorry. Making love with you *is* addictive. Will anyone notice if my truck stays parked outside all night?"

She snuggled against him, not caring about anyone or anything except the man beside her. "Probably, but I don't mind, if you don't."

He kissed her forehead. "I can't imagine being anywhere else."

CHAPTER ELEVEN

ZACH WOKE at five, as usual. What wasn't usual was waking with a beautiful woman in his arms. He lay quietly, taking care not to disturb Leslie as he shifted to ease the cramp in his neck.

The night had been short as far as sleep was concerned. They would have had even less, but from what Leslie had told him, Mondays were nightmarishly busy, and he hadn't wanted to wear her out before she went to work.

Sometime around midnight, he'd helped her shut off the lights and throw the front door dead bolt before they returned to her room. If he'd been thinking, he would have filled her coffeemaker so it would brew automatically before they got up, but he hadn't. He toyed with the idea of sliding out of bed, fixing a pot and crawling back in, but he hated to leave her, even for a few minutes. His next few evenings were filled with business commitments, so he wanted to make the most of his time with her.

Beside him, Leslie stirred, and he raised himself up on one elbow to watch her awaken. Her eyelids fluttered open, and he waited for her glimmer of recognition before he broke the predawn silence. "Good morning," he said softly.

A slow, come-hither smile crept across her face. "Good morning, yourself."

"I was going to fix coffee, but I didn't want to leave you for those few minutes."

"I'm glad you didn't. You would have been hunting for a coffeepot for a long time."

"You don't own one?" he guessed.

"Nope. It seems pointless to fix coffee here when I can drink all I want at the hospital."

"Then it's a good thing I decided to be lazy."

"Unfortunately, I have to rise and shine," she said apologetically. "I report for duty early because it smooths the transition between shifts. What are you doing today?"

"Since I'm in town, I'm going to stop at my parents' and see if I can beg some breakfast. Then it's back to the ranch. I have buyers coming the next two evenings, so I need to get my paperwork in order."

"Then you'll be busy."

"Afraid so. Some guys are all business, and we're done within an hour. Others, like the fellow who's coming tonight, notoriously arrive late and don't know when to leave."

"That's too bad."

"Wednesday night isn't booked."

"I'll keep it open," she promised.

"Now that you've heard my schedule, what's on tap for you?"

She smiled coyly. "Healing the sick with my phenomenal skills and tender touch."

"You'd better save that tender touch for me," he teased.

"I will."

Through the window, he could see the sky begin to lighten, and he wished the sun would hold off its appearance for another hour or two. "What time did you say you have to be at work?"

"At six-thirty." She glanced at the clock and groaned. "Five more minutes."

He let her nestle against him. Although the midday temperature reached the upper seventies, mornings were still cool. "Take all the time you want," he said. Then, out of curiosity, he asked, "Do you always keep the night-light on?"

She stiffened. "Did it bother you?"

"No. I had more important things on my mind. I noticed it, that's all."

"It's an old habit. After I lost my husband and son, I started leaving the light on. I didn't feel quite so alone. Now it's become like an old friend."

He understood completely. "I left the radio on in the kitchen for the first few weeks after Monica moved out. I guess we all need something to help us get through that adjustment period."

"I couldn't have said it better." She stretched. "I really have to be going or I'll be late."

"You can shower first. If I drop in this early at my parents' town house, they'll ask questions that I'd rather not answer. Unless you don't mind if I tell them about us."

"Would it hurt your feelings if we kept this between ourselves for now?"

"No. Whatever makes you more comfortable." She'd taken a big step last night and she clearly needed time to regroup. Zach was more than willing to give her that time, as long as she wasn't talking years.

"Okay."

While Leslie disappeared in the bathroom, he pulled on his clothes and flexed his shoulder, aware of the twinge across his back. Because he was hungry, he searched around and found a bag of blueberry bagels in the bread box. She obviously didn't cook much because her cupboards were empty and her refrigerator was in desperate need of restocking.

Thirty minutes later, she dashed into the kitchen. "Gotta run," she said. "I'll be late."

"Have a bagel," he ordered. "It's all I could find."

"That's more than I usually have for breakfast. Thanks."

He shook his head. "I thought doctors were supposed to be nutrition fanatics."

"We are. I usually—"

He held up his hands. "Don't tell me. You usually grab something at the hospital."

In answer, she smiled as she took a bite.

He leaned over and kissed her cheek. "Maybe it's time you learned a new routine."

"I will," she promised.

"If you don't mind, I think I'll go through Rose's file again before I leave. Maybe we missed a vital piece of information."

"Be my guest. It's on the desk in my office. Now, I really have to go. Help yourself to whatever you need."

The moment Leslie swept from the house, he felt her absence. After a quick shower, he found the file in her office, lying next to a framed family photo. Surrounded by her husband and son, Leslie appeared so happy. He'd wanted a glimpse of her before the tragedy, and this picture showed how vital and full of life she'd been. To most people she might seem that way now, but Zach could see the shadows in her eyes and wanted to remove them completely.

He sat down and went through Rose's chart again,

but no clues jumped out at him. By the time he finished, it was a decent enough hour to arrive at his parents' house without raising their curiosity, so he headed in that direction.

Should he tell them what he'd discovered? Heaven knew, his feelings for them hadn't changed a bit. The skills they'd taught him, the morals they'd instilled in him, the closeness they'd cultivated made them his parents, regardless of their lack of a blood tie.

Leslie's advice was sound, he thought as he drove into their gated community. He'd play things by ear until he had a chance to talk to Zane and get his input. In the meantime, he'd find out as much as he could about Rose and the man in her life.

The front door stood open and he knocked once before walking in. ''Anybody home?'' he called, finding his parents in the kitchen.

''Zach,'' Eleanor exclaimed. ''How nice to see you. What brings you to town so early?''

''Odds and ends,'' he said. ''Is that coffee I smell?''

''Decaf,'' his father grumbled. ''How that's supposed to help a man get a jump-start on his day is beyond me.''

''Hamilton,'' Eleanor chided. ''You know what the doctor told you. Cut down on your salt and your caffeine.''

''I know, I know. Help yourself, Zach. The more you drink, the less I will.''

Zach poured a cup and sat at the table.

''Would you like bacon and eggs for breakfast?'' his mother asked as she poked around in her refrigerator.

''Only if you're fixing them for Dad,'' he said, eyeing his father's bowl of granola flakes. ''Otherwise, I'll stick to cereal.''

"Eat the good stuff while you can, son," Hamilton said. "When you get to be my age, if it tastes good, the doctors won't let you have it."

"Don't be silly," Eleanor chided, clearly used to Hamilton's grousing. "Maybe if I hadn't fed you so well when you were younger, you wouldn't have heart problems now. Let this be a lesson to you, Zach."

Hamilton leaned closer. "Don't pay attention to your mother," he said in a loud whisper. "It's a good thing you're not married. At least you can still eat what you want without the little woman watching every bite you take."

Eleanor sat beside her husband and took his ribbing with a good-natured smile. "Now, Hamilton. If you're going to give me grief about breakfast, you'll get ground turkey for dinner instead of ground beef."

Hamilton winked at Zach. "Yes, dear."

Zach smiled at his parents. He'd hoped his marriage with Monica would be like theirs, but sadly, it hadn't worked out that way. Perhaps, if he decided to take the plunge again, he'd be luckier.

"And speaking of the little woman," Eleanor said as she dipped her spoon into her own bowl of granola. "We've been hearing stories about you."

"Really? Like what?"

"That you're seeing some lady at the hospital. A doctor."

Word certainly traveled fast. "I've taken Leslie Hall out a few times," he admitted. "She's Walter Keller's daughter, you know."

"Really? I hadn't heard that," Eleanor said thoughtfully.

"Yeah, well, I'm not sure she wants it to be common knowledge. Walter was so well known and loved around here, it must be tough to follow in his footsteps.''

"How true. Still…'' His mother hesitated.

"Still what?'' Zach coaxed, sensing that he wouldn't like the news she was about to share.

"Now, you know we wouldn't interfere in your life,'' Eleanor said. "But we're worried about you.''

"What for?''

"What your mother is trying to say,'' Hamilton interrupted, "is that she's afraid you're going to fall for her and get hurt.''

"Why would you think that?''

"A friend of mine has a daughter who works at the West View Hospital. She says that this Dr. Hall is here under some very shady circumstances.''

Zach leaned back in his chair, his mind whirling with possibilities. "Like what?''

"Well, there's a gap of about a year in her employment record. It's like she disappeared and no one knows where she went.''

"When?'' he asked.

"Two years ago.''

The date made sense. "Her husband and son were killed. I know she had a hard time dealing with it. She probably took time off.''

"If that's the case, then why the secrecy? And why is her probation twice as long as for other new doctors?''

"I don't know, Mom,'' he admitted.

"She hasn't told you?''

"No.'' He thought of their conversation last night. *There are things you don't know about me.*

"I'm telling you, Zach,'' Eleanor continued, "if she's keeping things from you, then be wary. You don't need to get involved with another woman who has a secret life.''

"We know how lonely a man can get," Hamilton said. "Just don't start thinking with your hormones instead of your head."

"Thanks for the warning," Zach said wryly. "It's duly noted."

"But, Zach," Eleanor added, "that's not all."

He raised an eyebrow. "There's more?"

"People think she may have spent that year in a mental institution."

He stared at his parents, incredulous, before anger set in. "That's a horrible accusation to make. Do they have any proof?"

Eleanor exchanged a glance with Hamilton. "I don't think so...."

"See?" Zach said triumphantly. "I can't believe you're falling for a story that someone with an overactive imagination dreamed up to add a little spice to their life. Leslie is a quiet person, but just because she isn't a social butterfly doesn't mean she's crazy.

"She's gentle, understanding and one of the most levelheaded people I've met. I'm proud to say that I know her." At the end of his defense, he stopped himself from admitting what he'd just realized. He loved her.

Unfortunately, his parents weren't ready to hear that. Nor was he about to tell them before he told Leslie.

"Oh, Zach," Eleanor said. "We only want you to be careful. That's all."

"I know you're looking out for me and I respect that," he said. "But until she tells me this herself, I'm not going to believe it." He didn't doubt that she had secrets, but surely if they were of this magnitude, she'd trust him enough to bring them into the open.

Wouldn't she?

AFTER A NIGHT spent in the clouds, walking into the ER was a startling jolt back to earth. The department was already humming with activity, with everything from ringing phones and crying babies to staff members rushing around as they hurried to keep pace with the onslaught of cases waiting for their attention.

The sight of every tall, dark-haired man reminded her of Zach, and thinking of him brought a smile to her face throughout the entire day.

"Whew," Betty said as she signed off on her last chart. "We must have set a new record."

"Definitely," Leslie agreed.

"What I want to know is, why do you look as fresh as a daisy and the rest of us look like we've been pulled through a knothole? You worked as hard as we did, so what gives?"

Leslie wasn't about to explain that Zach had given her a new lease on life. "You're imagining things."

Betty shook her head. "Believe me. I know perky when I see it, and you are definitely still perky."

Leslie shrugged and hid her smile. "It's all in the genes."

"Aha," Betty exclaimed. "Genes are right—although I think you're referring to denim and not chromosomes."

Leslie's face warmed. "You're jumping to conclusions."

"Oh, no, I'm not," Betty said, her eyes twinkling. "You're seeing Zach Dumas."

"We've spent time together, yes."

"You know something? You are the absolute queen of the understatement."

"I am not."

"Yes, you are, you sly thing," Betty crooned.

"It's really nothing to get excited over," she said, trying to throw Betty off the trail of a juicy tidbit. "We've gone to dinner a few times and enjoyed each other's company. End of story."

"Uh-huh. I have a feeling this story is just beginning. One of these days, you're going to wake up with his boots under your bed."

Since the nurse's words had struck remarkably close to home, Leslie decided to appeal to her sense of fair play. "Look, I'm not sure where this is going between us, so if you don't mind, I'd rather not let it become common knowledge."

Betty patted her hand as she bestowed a huge grin on her. "You got it, Doc. I understand completely. You don't want to jinx anything. I was the same way with my first few guys. Then after a while—" she waved her hand "—it didn't matter. Don't worry. If word leaks out, it won't be on account of me. I'm the soul of secrecy."

Leslie wasn't sure she agreed with Betty's self-analysis, but she didn't argue. "Thanks," she said.

However, as she went home, she knew that regardless of what Zach had said about forgetting the past and starting over, at some point she would have to tell him about the worst year of her life. He'd entrusted his secrets to her, and she should do the same, especially now that she found herself falling in love with him.

He made her feel as if she'd been granted a second chance at happiness, and she was reluctant to do or say anything that might rip that opportunity out of her grasp. Yet she had to be honest. Her secret wasn't the same as the one her father had kept. Too many people, however trustworthy they were, knew of her past, or at least enough of it to fill in the blanks. Far better for him to hear the news from her than from someone else.

She would tell him, she decided. The next time she saw him. If everything fell apart, then so be it. At least she had one night to remember.

As she walked inside her home and strolled into her bedroom, his presence filled every corner of every room. His fragrance hung in the air, reminding her of the hours he'd spent with her. Who was she kidding? One night wasn't nearly enough.

She'd left that morning with the bed unmade, his pillow indented with the shape of his head. Now the quilt covered it, although it hung over the sides unevenly. She smiled at his thoughtful attempt. Perhaps she'd teach him how to make hospital corners after they tangled the sheets with more pleasurable activities.

With one last, longing glance at the bed, she changed clothes and went into the kitchen. A brand-new two-cup coffeemaker, complete with a timer, stood on the counter. She'd assumed he would be back, but his gift seemed to confirm it.

You have to tell him, that little voice demanded.

''I will,'' she said aloud. *When the subject comes up,* she amended. Divulging her past wasn't something that she could do out of the blue. When the time was right, she'd be completely honest and let the chips fall where they may.

With a happy heart, she took care of a few household chores until she finally sat down to quilt as she watched the six o'clock news. Her thoughts kept straying to Zach instead of focusing on her stitching, and after ripping out several crooked seams, she gave up.

He'd wanted more information about Rose, and since he hadn't left a note, she presumed that he hadn't found anything. At least digging through files and hunting for clues would keep her from listening—hoping—for the phone to ring.

Setting aside Rose's medical chart, Leslie turned instead to her father's business records. Someone had to have paid Rose's bill, even though she'd died. Several hours later, she found a name.

"Lisa Castaldo," she read from the bound invoice. Lisa's address and a faded red Paid in Full stamp marked the invoice for services rendered to one Rose Rydic.

She dashed upstairs to the phone book, hoping to find a listing. One Castaldo caught her eye, but it belonged to Gordon. Was this Lisa's husband? The address didn't match, but they could have moved. She punched in the number to find out, hoping the household she was calling didn't go to bed early.

The voice at the other end was male and sounded elderly. "My name is Dr. Leslie Hall, and I'm sorry for phoning so late," she began, "but I'm looking for a Lisa Castaldo. Does she live here?"

"Lisa died several years ago," he said.

"I'm sorry to hear that." Leslie was sorrier than the man could know. "Are you her husband?"

He chuckled. "Oh, my, no. Lisa was too independent to hitch herself to a fella. She was my sister."

Leslie's disappointment at reaching a dead end turned to excitement.

"Actually, a friend and I are looking for information

about a woman who stayed with your sister nearly forty years ago.''

''I'd be happy to help you, but I didn't know many of Lisa's boarders. She took people in like some folks take in stray cats, but she had a huge house on her ranch and liked the company. I had enough on my plate trying to keep track of my business associates and customers without worrying about Lisa's causes.''

''Really?'' She forced herself to sound calm, when inside she wanted to shout. ''What sort of business were you in?''

''I owned the Gold Nugget. It was a combination casino and nightclub. I retired about five years ago.''

Leslie closed her eyes, breathed a silent word of thanks and sagged against the counter. ''Then you might know the woman we're looking for. She was a singer.''

''Lots of pretty gals came through town trying to make their way by singing. Some stayed, and others moved on.''

''You may remember this one. Her name was Rose. Rose Rydic.''

Dead silence filled her ear. If she had heard a thump, she would have called an ambulance. ''Mr. Castaldo?'' she asked.

''I remember Rose.''

''My friend and I would like to talk to you about her. Would you mind if we visited you Wednesday night?'' Zach had said he was free, so she felt safe making plans.

''Sure. I'd be happy to talk. I don't get much company these days.''

Leslie disconnected the call and immediately dialed Zach's number. News like this couldn't wait, regardless if he *was* in the middle of a business deal.

The phone rang and rang and rang. "Come on, Zach. Pick up," she urged.

She was ready to disconnect when his voice came over the wire. "Dumas," he barked.

"Oh, Zach," she said. "I'm sorry to interrupt but I have the most marvelous news."

"Leslie?"

"Yeah. I found her."

"Who?"

"Lisa Castaldo. Rose's landlady and the woman who paid her hospital bill. Actually, she's dead, but her brother, Gordon, isn't. He's the man who hired Rose to work in his casino."

LESLIE SMILED at the elderly gentleman seated across from her and Zach on the sofa in the drawing room. Gordon Castaldo wasn't anything like she expected. Instead of a man who got by on a modest retirement income, he wore designer clothes and lived in a mansion. Clearly, owning a casino had proven to be a lucrative career. Although he had to be in his late seventies, he still had a full head of white hair. In spite of his outward trappings of wealth, his speech reflected more humble roots.

"As I explained to you on the phone, Mr. Castaldo..." she began.

He waved a hand that hardly seemed strong enough to lift the huge ring on his finger. "Please, call me Gordon."

"Thank you, Gordon. As I was saying, we're trying to track down information on Rose Rydic. We've been told that she might have worked for you."

"Oh, yes, she did. I remember her as plain as if I'd

just seen her yesterday. But why the interest in Rose? She's been gone nearly forty years.''

Leslie wasn't certain how much of Zach's story he wanted to tell. Before she could reply, Zach took over.

''We discovered that she was my mother,'' Zach answered smoothly. ''She had twins before she died.''

Gordon's bushy eyebrows drew together. ''Twins? I understood the baby died with her.''

Leslie had anticipated his questions and had prepared her answer. ''Since Rose was an unwed mother without any family, the doctor felt it was in the babies' best interests to go to a loving couple after she died. You might say it was a private adoption.''

''I see. Well, it was probably just as well,'' he said. ''So what did you want to know about her?''

He'd accepted her explanation without batting an eyelash, and Leslie released the breath she'd been holding. ''Everything.''

He smiled. ''That, I'm afraid, won't take long to tell. Nearly forty years ago, I got a picture and a cassette recording in the mail. I'd get hundreds of them, but hers stood out. When I heard her sing, it brought tears to my eyes. I offered her a job, and she arrived a week later. As soon as she stepped off the plane, I knew that if she was half as good as she looked, I had a winner.''

''When was this?'' Zach asked.

''March first. I remember because it was my birthday, and oh, what a present she turned out to be. She wanted to earn her keep, so I scheduled her to sing that Friday. Within days, my business boomed. It became standing room only.''

''She was that good?'' Leslie asked.

''She was the best. I'm not just saying that, either.

I've seen a lot of talented musicians, but she was fantastic.''

Leslie glanced at Zach and saw a small smile on his face. Pride, perhaps? She listened as Gordon continued.

''Like I was saying, in no time at all, she was the newest and hottest singing sensation in Reno. Her sultry voice just seemed to drive men wild. I had to hire extra security guards to keep the more enthusiastic fellows from making a nuisance of themselves.''

''How did she take her notoriety?'' Leslie asked.

''She thrived on it,'' he said. ''She had dreams of going to California and making an album, but she said she wanted the experience of singing in a club. I was more than happy to keep her as long as she wanted to stay.''

''What did you do when you found out she was pregnant?'' Leslie asked.

''She told me about a month after she started. I knew her days of appearing in front of a crowd were numbered. I thought she'd sing for a few months and then take a leave until after the baby was born, but she insisted on working as long as possible.''

Leslie couldn't visualize a pregnant woman performing in a nightclub, even if she had a great voice. ''What did you do?''

''We turned the stage into a set that looked like a saloon during the gold rush days, and enclosed the balcony so folks could only see Rose's head and shoulders. She was a looker, and we couldn't hide her completely without causing an uproar. Anyway, to draw some of the attention off herself, Rose suggested we bring in dancers. The customers loved it.''

''It sounds as if Rose had a flair for pleasing an audience.'' No wonder Zach had taken to performing in his school musicals as if he was born to the task, Leslie thought.

"Oh, my, yes. It broke my heart when I heard she died. The entire entertainment industry in Reno was shocked, I don't mind telling you."

"Did she ever mention a boyfriend? The father of her baby?" Zach asked.

"Not to me, she didn't. It couldn't have been anyone local."

"Why not?" Leslie asked.

"For one thing, she didn't go out with anyone. For another, she arrived in March, and her baby was born in October. I may be old, but I can still count, and that doesn't add up to nine months."

Leslie knew that multiple-birth pregnancies didn't always go full-term, but considering how healthy Zach and Zane had been, Rose probably delivered fairly close to her due date.

"I figure she was already in the family way when she walked off that plane."

Zach leaned forward. "Where was she from?"

"She never said much about her past, but her flight arrived from Boston."

Leslie gripped Zach's hand. They were slowly but surely unraveling the strands of the mystery, and she was excited for him.

"Massachusetts?"

"I don't know of any other. Come to think of it, I kept a box of her things. I cleaned out her dressing room and saved some of her stuff, including some of her tapes, in case any of her family ever came looking for her. No one ever did. Would you like to see them?"

Zach's eyes lit up like a marquee. "Yes. Please."

Gordon opened a built-in cabinet on the far side of

the room and removed a nondescript shoe box. Returning to them, he removed the lid and took out a picture.

For a long moment, he stared at Zach, then the photo. "I was afraid you were pulling my leg, young man, but you certainly do carry a look of your mother about you."

CHAPTER TWELVE

ZACH STUDIED the upper-body shot of a woman as she stood behind a microphone in a red sequined dress. As Gordon had said, Rose Rydic was beautiful.

Gordon placed the box on the coffee table before he returned to his chair. "I really thought someone would look for her before now, but she must have cut her ties completely before she came out here. I kept all of her papers, though, just in case, including the copy of the death certificate. The funeral home gave it to us because we were the closest thing to kin she had."

Zach rummaged through the box. Underneath the two death certificates lay an ancient bottle of perfume, cosmetics, a billfold and several sequined hair clips. Near the bottom, he found an envelope stamped with an Official Use Only return address. With eager fingers, he pulled out the document it contained and could hardly believe his good fortune.

Leslie peered over his arm. "Oh, my gosh, Zach. You found Rose's birth record."

"This is so unbelievable." He scanned the typewritten details. "Her parents were Harold and Serena Rydic. She was born in Boston, Massachusetts." He looked at Leslie in near shock. "We're from the east coast."

"What else is in the box?" Leslie asked.

"Go ahead and look."

Zach memorized every detail of her birth certificate.

She was born on September fourteenth and was an only child. Had she left her parents behind, or had they died before she moved west?

The next two documents inside the envelope answered his question. They were the death certificates for Rose's parents. Serena had died of blood poisoning when Rose was young, while Harold, a fisherman, had drowned when she was eighteen.

Had Rose been left on her own, or were there other family members to turn to during this traumatic time? Was her dream of fame and fortune her means to escape obviously humble beginnings? There was no way to tell.

"It seems as if every answer only leads to more questions," he mused aloud.

Leslie pulled out a handful of photos from the very bottom and scanned them. "I know what you mean. These must be of Rose with her parents. I wonder who this guy is?"

Zach studied the black and white snapshot of Rose standing in the embrace of a young man who reminded Zach of himself.

"This is my father," he said.

"How can you be sure?" Leslie wanted to know.

"Look at him."

Leslie studied the photo. "You're right. He does look like you. Or you look like him. Whatever." She flipped it over. "It's a shame she didn't write his name on the back."

"Yeah. That would have been too easy." He took the photo and studied the background for clues. "Doesn't this building look like one you'd see on a campus? If I'm not mistaken, this is the top part of a sign."

Leslie glanced at the area he'd indicated. "Darn! The name isn't clear."

"I'll bet if we walk around the campus, we'll find this building."

"How do we know which campus to visit? There are thousands of colleges back east."

"We start with Boston University. If Rose's voice made her stand out in Reno, I'll bet the same thing happened in her hometown. Someone's bound to know something." He couldn't wait to begin.

He turned to Gordon. "I can't thank you enough for saving these. Anyone else would have thrown them out long ago."

"I couldn't," Gordon said simply. "She was special. Before I forget, I have one other thing you might be interested in seeing." He rose and went to another cabinet. "Lisa started a scrapbook of Rose's career at the Gold Nugget. She saved the newspaper articles and the entertainment reviews."

He pulled out a large black book and carried it over to them. "You're welcome to keep this, but I would ask one favor."

"Anything," Zach said as he began flipping through the pages of yellowed newspaper clippings and grainy photos. From the headlines, it was obvious Rose had been a popular attraction.

"Could you make a copy for me? Sometimes an old man likes to stroll down memory lane, if you know what I mean."

Zach nodded, touched by Gordon's generosity. "Yes, I do, and yes, I'll make a copy for you."

"Thank you." He paused for a fraction of a second before he continued offhandedly. "I was fifteen years older than Rose, but I offered to marry her—to give her baby a name.''

"What did she say?'' Leslie asked.

"She thanked me but said she couldn't because it wouldn't be fair to me. Maybe she was right. After knowing her, though, no other woman ever measured up. She was such a classy lady.''

"Then you've never married?'' Leslie asked.

He shook his head. "I guess I was like Rose. I couldn't settle for second-best.''

Zach held the book reverently. "Thanks for this. I'll send your copy over as soon as it's ready.''

"You do that. Did I understand you correctly? You're going to try to hunt down the fellow in this picture?''

"Yes.''

"When you do, if he doesn't have a good reason for letting her jet across the country, then punch him in the nose for me, will you?''

Zach smiled. "I'll keep your suggestion in mind.''

With the precious keepsakes on Leslie's lap, Zach drove to her house, hardly able to take in his good fortune. "This seems so unreal,'' he said.

"I know. It's almost as if someone upstairs is leading you in the right direction.''

"It's amazing, isn't it?''

"Did you notice how Gordon's voice changed when he talked about Rose? He was in love with her.''

"That was my impression, too.''

"Just think. You could have learned the ins and outs of gambling while singing for your supper.''

Zach tried to imagine growing up in the entertainment industry rather than the ranching business. Would he have become the man he was today under those circumstances? Somehow, he didn't think so.

"Now, that's a scary scenario," he said. "I'm glad I grew up where I did."

"Then you're not angry with my father anymore?"

"No. However things worked out, I'm thankful that Eleanor and Hamilton raised Zane and me. If your father were here, I'd tell him so."

Leslie's eyes glimmered. "I'm glad. And I'm sure he knows how you feel."

"He probably does." With that burden lifted, Zach realized it had been hours since he'd eaten. "Are you hungry?"

"Now? It's nearly nine o'clock."

"I know, but I haven't eaten since lunch. Things got hectic this afternoon, and I skipped dinner so we wouldn't be late."

"I'm not starving, but I could probably nibble on something. Wouldn't you rather grab takeout so you can go through Rose's things again?"

"A few hours won't change the treasures in the box. My stomach will divorce me if it has to wait any longer."

He drove to a country and western bar on the edge of town and pulled into the near-empty parking lot. It was a nondescript wooden structure, and a variety of neon beer logos hung in the front windows.

"McCornick and Weston," she read off the sign. "What is this?"

"A place that serves the best beef around."

Inside, he guided her past the bar to a vinyl-cushioned booth. He held up his hand at the waitress, who was wearing jeans and a red gingham shirt. "Two beers."

"Gotcha."

"This is quite the place," Leslie said as she glanced around.

Zach knew without looking that the rough cedar walls were adorned with horseshoes, spurs, lassos and an assortment of other western gear. "Yeah. It feels like home."

"Come here often, do you?" she teased.

"No, it's just nice to casually drop in somewhere for a beer. With the sawdust on the floor, no one worries about having clean shoes. On the weekends, they have a live country and western band and things really rock around here." He grinned. "Want to play a game of pool?"

"I don't know how."

"Then I'll teach you." Showing her how to properly hold a pool cue would make for an interesting evening. Lucky for him, the tables were free.

After the waitress delivered their bottles and took his order for a thick hamburger with all the trimmings, he decided it was time to begin the lessons.

"This isn't a good idea," she protested as he took her hand and drew her out of the booth toward the east side of the room, where two pool tables stood.

"Of course it is," he said, handing her a cue. "There's no time like the present."

She grabbed it. "Okay. Now what?"

He racked the balls and placed the white ball on the opposite end of the table. "Watch how I do this." Leaning over the table, he broke. Balls scattered across the table, some dropping into the pockets, others bouncing off the sides. "See how easy it is?"

"Yeah, right."

"Because more solid balls than striped balls fell in,

the solids are mine and the striped ones are yours. Now, look at this one.'' He pointed to the far right pocket, and a yellow-striped ball that stood within three inches of it. ''Aim here.''

She leaned across the table, and Zach stood over her. Placing his left hand over hers, he positioned her hand to guide the cue. Then, reaching around her, he covered her right hand with his and made a few practice motions.

''Do you have the feel of it?'' he asked. If she didn't, he certainly did. His blood was roaring through his body as fast as water rushing off the Rockies during spring melt. Finishing this game would take supreme willpower on his part.

Did she have the feel of it? Leslie felt more than he probably intended her to feel, but it was delightful to have his arms around her. She had an idea she'd be a student who would require a lot of personal attention to master this game.

''I think so,'' she said.

''Let 'er rip.''

Although he still kept his hands on her, she took control. She punched at the white ball and it hopped, completely missing her target. ''Darn.''

''No problem. Now, aim for the solid red.''

''But it's yours.''

''I know. I'll do the work. I just want you to get the technique down.''

Although he leaned over her once again, this time, he delivered the thrust that sent the ball careening into a side pocket.

Leslie didn't mind playing the entire game with his arms around her, whether it was her turn or not. It wasn't until he got ready to sink the eight ball on his last shot that she noticed one of the other customers watching them from his table.

He was a sandy-haired fellow in his late twenties who looked like a financial analyst on his way home from work. The top button of his dress shirt was open, and his tie hung loosely at his neck. At first, she thought he'd wallowed in a few too many drinks, but when she caught his gaze, his eyes seemed remarkably clear.

He raised his glass ever so slightly in a silent toast, and a shiver crawled down her spine. Fortunately, Zach ended the game and they headed to their table.

"Don't look now," she told him, "but do you know the guy back there?"

Zach turned to slide in the booth and glanced at the man she'd indicated. "No. Why?"

She shrugged, unable to explain her uneasiness. "He watched me while we were playing pool."

"Why wouldn't he? You're the most beautiful woman here tonight."

"Other than the waitress, I'm the *only* woman here," she said dryly.

"Ah, he was probably just thinking he'd like to be in my shoes."

She didn't agree, but rather than create an issue, she dropped the subject. Fortunately, the waitress brought Zach's meal at that moment.

While he dug into his hamburger, she helped herself to a few of the French fries in his overflowing basket.

"Are you ready for a trip to Boston?" he asked.

"That depends."

"On what?"

"When you're planning to go," she said. "Everyone wants to take their vacations in June."

"Let's leave in two weeks," he said.

"I'm not sure I can get away on such short notice," she warned.

"Try."

"Won't you have the boys then?"

"We'll work it out. I'll have them this weekend, and I want you to spend Saturday with us at the ranch," he said.

"Camping?"

'Not this time. We're going to hang around home. I need to start organizing things if I'll be gone for a week."

"I'll be in the way if you're working," she informed him. "My experience with cattle is limited to what shows up on my plate."

"Then it will be a new experience. I wouldn't worry. We'll find something for you to do. For supper, I'll throw hamburgers and hot dogs on the grill and we can watch the sunset." He grinned. "This time, from the back porch. Next time, from my secret hideaway."

"Sounds like fun. What shall I bring?"

"Just yourself."

"BETTY, you have to help me." Leslie grabbed the younger woman on Friday morning and led her away from the nurses' station toward her office.

"With what?"

"I'm going to a barbecue and I'd like to contribute to the meal, but I don't know what to bring."

"Who's coming and what's being served?"

"Zach and his two boys. Hamburgers and hot dogs."

Betty elbowed her. "Zach and his boys, eh? Sounds a little cozy to me."

Leslie rolled her eyes. She'd expected Betty to react like this, but desperation had motivated her to swallow her pride and ask for her advice anyway. "Betty, I need help," she said crisply, "not adolescent humor."

"Okay, okay. Let's see. Well, guys like food that sticks to their ribs. Your Zach sounds like a meat-and-potatoes kind of guy."

"I thought about rice."

Betty grimaced.

"What about a vegetable tray?"

The nurse pantomimed a gag. "Kids and vegetables don't go together."

Leslie threw up her hands. "Then what?" She'd pored over her recipe files, but nothing seemed right.

"Try spaghetti salad. Kids, especially boys, love to slurp spaghetti, so they'll have fun while they're eating. It's also simple to make." She recited the recipe, which called for cooked spaghetti and a bottle of Italian dressing.

"That's it?"

"Sure. I told you it was simple. Oh, and don't break the pasta before you dump it in the hot water. The longer the strands, the better for slurping."

"How do you know these things?"

"I have three brothers. I could tell you more, but I wouldn't want to scare you."

"I appreciate it," Leslie said dryly.

"Is there any other advice you might need?" Betty winked.

"Not at the moment, but thanks."

"Okay." Betty turned to go, then stopped to face her once again. "You know something? You've changed."

Leslie tensed. "What do you mean?"

The nurse shrugged. "You're more relaxed. More friendly."

"I've always been friendly."

"You've been polite and treated us as equals," Betty said in her forthright manner, "but now you're different. Softer. Let's face it. You wouldn't have asked any of us for advice before."

It was true. Leslie had discouraged any overtures of friendship from her first day on the job.

"Anyway, you're really a nice person," Betty continued. She smiled. "Since I suspect that Zach brought about your metamorphosis, I'll give you another piece of advice. Hang on to this dude."

Leslie grinned. "I'll do my best."

LESLIE ARRIVED at Zach's ranch to find it seemingly deserted. Although the barn door stood open, Zach's disreputable truck was missing. Only the sound of an occasional moo broke the early-afternoon silence.

She carried her bowl of spaghetti salad into the house and stopped in surprise. Zach's home hardly resembled its former pristine self. Boxes, toys and an assortment of other gear lay in every room. The only neat area of the house was the kitchen, and its sink was filled to overflowing with dirty dishes.

Clearly, Zach's boys had arrived.

Deciding to make herself useful, she began washing the tableware. By the time she'd shelved the last cup and saucer, the front door burst open and the sound of a stampede greeted her.

"Boys," she heard Zach say sternly, "we walk in the house. We don't run."

"Okay, Dad," the youthful voices echoed as they came to a dead stop in the kitchen. Leslie waited for the familiar pang to strike her, but this time, it didn't hit her with the same harsh intensity. Seeing these two made Brandon's memory more bittersweet than painful.

Her therapist had assured her that she would always bear the scars but time would heal the wounds. Perhaps the process had finally begun.

Zach was one step behind and he grinned at her. "Hi, Leslie. Have you been here long?"

"Long enough to tidy up the breakfast and dinner dishes," she said.

"You didn't have to do that."

She shrugged. "I know. I don't mind."

Zach nudged the boys forward. "Where are your manners?"

"Hi, Dr. Hall," they greeted her.

Leslie glanced at the boys, who were dressed alike today. She crossed her fingers as she addressed each one by name. "Hi, Keith. It's nice to see you again, Kenny."

The boys' mouths dropped open, and their eyes widened as they first looked at her, then at each other. "How could you tell us apart?" they wanted to know.

She smiled. "I have my ways."

Keith seemed skeptical while Kenny continued to stare at her in awe. "That's the best part of being twins," Keith complained. "Being able to fool people."

"Well, you can't fool me," she said.

"Which is a good thing, because you'll see Leslie a lot," he told the boys.

"We will?" Kenny asked.

Zach nodded. "Not every day, but often enough."

Keith narrowed his eyes slightly. "Are you going to boss us around?"

Leslie sensed the lines of battle were being drawn. "Do you need to be bossed around?"

Both boys shook their heads.

"Then we shouldn't have a problem," she answered.

Apparently Keith wasn't completely convinced, because he continued firing questions. "Are you going to make us wash our hands before we eat?"

"*I* intend to do that," Zach answered.

"What about eating vegetables and not letting us have dessert first?"

"I hope you'll want to eat properly so you can grow as big and strong as your father, but if you don't want to, then—" she shrugged as if the subject was of little concern to her "—it's up to you."

"Are you going to tell Dad we can't do things, like ride the bulls and wrestle steers?" Kenny asked.

Leslie managed to hide her smile. "When your dad says you're strong enough to ride bulls and rope calves, then I'll trust his judgment. Of course, if you don't eat your vegetables, it may take a long time until then. Oh, Kenny, I wanted to tell you what a good job you did when the fishhook hurt your dad. If you want any first-aid tips for next time, I'll be happy to share a few of my tricks with you."

Kenny's eyes lit with interest. "Cool."

"One thing I will be bossy about, though," she said, noticing how Keith's suspicious face had reappeared. "You must promise your dad that you will never, ever, *ever* touch the guns in the gun cabinet unless he's with you. I want to visit you here at the ranch, not have you visit me in the hospital because you shot yourselves. Is it a deal?"

"Yeah," they echoed.

"Dad already made us promise," Kenny added.

"I'm glad."

Zach placed one hand on each of their shoulders and turned them in the direction of their bedroom. "Go on and organize your gear while Leslie and I discuss dinner.''

The two boys tramped off, jostling each other in Keith's rush to be first.

''How can you tell them apart?'' Zach asked her.

''Keith's the oldest, right?''

He nodded. ''By about twenty minutes.''

''I thought so. He's the first one in the car, the first one in the kitchen, and just now—'' she motioned ''—he was the first one down the hall. He's also more skeptical, more of a plotter. I can see it in his eyes.''

''You pegged him right,'' Zach said.

''As for Kenny, he's the quieter of the two. He seems to follow Keith's lead, and he's also more tenderhearted.''

''Yes, he is.''

''I rest my case.''

''You're fantastic.''

''I know.'' She grinned. ''It's nice to know that other people think so, too.''

Suddenly, she found herself in his arms, being swung around the room. ''Zach,'' she protested, laughing. ''What are you doing?''

''You're not going to believe this,'' he said, setting her on her feet but not relinquishing his hold. ''Monica has let the boys move in with me.''

''She's what?''

He nodded, his green eyes shining with undisguised excitement. ''Apparently, she was asked to join a big, upscale catering firm in Seattle. With the hours she'll be working and the fact that she didn't want to totally uproot the boys, she's agreed to let them spend the summer here. If the boys want to stay for school in the fall, she's willing to oblige.''

That explained the boxes in the living room. "Oh, Zach," Leslie said, returning his hug. "This is what you've wanted. I'm so happy for you."

"I'm rather surprised she agreed," he admitted. "Apparently she's wanted this job for a long time and jumped at the chance when they offered it."

"But to let you keep the boys..." Leslie wondered if she could have given her children into an ex-husband's care.

"She's wanted a job like this ever since I can remember. She doesn't care much for the business side of catering—she'd rather prepare the food. Anyway, she'll be working long hours, and she decided that it was time for me to look after the boys. I couldn't be happier."

"Just think of all the camping you'll get to do," she teased. "Maybe I should buy you a suit of armor for your fishing trips."

"With a doctor along, I won't need it."

His comment made her realize that they'd rarely have an opportunity to be alone. It also occurred to her that his quest for his roots might take a back seat to full-time parenthood.

"What about the trip to Boston?" she asked. "I made arrangements for someone to cover my shifts the week after next."

"We're still going," he said. "I've already warned Monica that I would be out of town, and my parents have agreed to stay here with the boys. With Melinda and her two only a few miles down the road, Keith and Kenny won't know I'm gone."

"If you're sure."

He pulled her close. "I am. Having the boys may

require some adjustments as far as we're concerned, but we'll work it out.''

She smiled, but her smile didn't reflect the heaviness in her heart. His greatest desire was to have his boys with him, and she couldn't do anything to ruin that privilege. He might take the news of her time in a private psychiatric hospital in stride, but she wondered if his ex-wife would be as understanding, especially where her children were concerned.

Leslie braced herself to tell her story. "Remember when I said that there were things you didn't know about me?''

"Yeah, so?''

"Well, maybe it's time you—''

Keith and Kenny burst into the room, their boot heels clattering against the linoleum. "Dad. You gotta come. Kenny's hamster got loose and he ran behind the washing machine.''

"I thought you boys promised not to let Oscar out of his cage unless your door was shut.''

"It was,'' Kenny insisted.

"Was not,'' Keith responded.

"It was only open a crack,'' Kenny defended. "I didn't think he could sneak through.''

"Told you he would,'' Keith accused.

"Boys,'' Zach ordered in a firm tone. "Let's quit arguing and find the hamster before the dog does.'' Casting an apologetic, what-else-can-I-do look in Leslie's direction, Zach went on his hamster hunt.

Leslie's moment passed. She wasn't sure if she was glad for the reprieve or sad because now she had to build her courage again.

She stayed on the alert for the rest of the day, in case another opportunity arose. It never did, but as the afternoon turned into evening, she recognized how precious Zach's boys were, even when they spilled their drinks, poked olives on each finger before they ate them and slurped the spaghetti.

She also fell more in love with Zach. His patience with their endless questions, their constant motion and the occasional fight reinforced her opinion that he was a true family man.

Someday, perhaps she, too, could become an integral part of his inner circle. In the meantime, she'd make the most of each day and store up another set of precious memories.

CHAPTER THIRTEEN

"THIS IS IT." Zach double-checked the house number on the three-story brownstone apartment building. It matched the one on the envelope containing the official birth and death certificates of Rose and her parents.

Leslie stood beside him on the step. "Do you want to ring the bell, or shall I?"

He answered by pressing the buzzer. The past ten days had been filled with activity. Not only had he tried to settle the boys in their former home and reestablish his authority as a full-time parent, but he'd had to organize his ranch affairs with his foreman for the time he would be gone. His days had been full, his nights short, and he'd barely found a moment to breathe until he boarded the plane.

He hadn't realized how nerve-racking his search in Boston was going to be until he left the airport and found himself in the middle of a traffic jam that exceeded anything he could have imagined. Fortunately, he had Leslie to turn to, and even if their trip didn't yield any information, he could at least claim one success. He had Leslie to himself for five glorious days and nights.

Another bell finally buzzed, indicating the lock had been released. Before it stopped its jarring noise, he opened the door and waited for Leslie to step inside. The first door on the right bore a sign labeled Manager, and he ushered her across the threshold into what appeared a typical office.

Two stainless steel file cabinets stood against one wall within close proximity to a matching gray metal desk. A spider plant hung over a bookcase under the east window. Several huge telephone books and volumes of the Yellow Pages rested on the shelves, although most of the case was filled with knickknacks and bird figurines.

"May I help you?" A woman in her fifties, with strands of silver in her dark curly hair, sat behind the desk. Zach decided that she was probably too young to be of any help, but he had to ask.

He stepped forward. "Have you owned this apartment building long?"

"For five years," she said.

His hopes sank. From Leslie's expression, it looked as if she thought this was a dead end, too.

"I took over when my parents passed away. Why?"

His hopes slowly rose once more. "I wonder if you could help us," he began. "I'm looking for a woman who lived at this address about forty years ago."

"I grew up in this house, and we had more renters than I could count. I'm afraid that ninety percent of them didn't stick in my mind," she apologized.

He reached in his pocket and held out the photo. "Perhaps this one did," he said, clinging to his hope. "The woman's name was Rose Rydic."

She glanced at the photo and instantly beamed. "Why, yes. I do remember her. Goodness, she's been gone since I was a little girl. At the time, I thought she was so sophisticated, but then someone in their twenties would seem that way to a thirteen-year-old."

"Did she live here long?"

"Several years. I'm not sure where she went, though."

"Can you tell us anything about her?" Leslie asked.

"Oh, yes. I loved it when she was at home. She worked nights, you know, and I was in school all day, so I didn't see her often. Her apartment was next to ours, and I always opened the windows so I could hear her sing. She was better than the people on the radio."

She smiled, remembering. "One time, it was freezing outside, but I couldn't make the words out to the song she was singing, so I put on my winter hat and coat and opened the window. I got in trouble and caught a cold, too, but it was worth it. Rose came to see me a few days later and gave me a piece of paper with the words. She was a special lady."

"Do you know where she worked?" Zach asked.

The woman shook her head. "If I did, I've forgotten. I'm sure it had to do with singing, though, because she practiced constantly."

"Is there anything else you can remember?" he pressed.

"Oh, yes. One year, I wanted to get my parents something special for Christmas, but I didn't have any money. Rose said she'd draw my picture, and she did. Everyone said it looked just like me, but then, everything she drew looked real. She had so much talent."

Her story confirmed what Zach had begun to suspect—his artistic bent came from his birth mother. He wished that he had some of her drawings, but he supposed they had disappeared over the years.

"Did any of her friends visit?" Leslie asked.

The woman grew thoughtful. "Not that I can remember."

"Then the man in the photo isn't familiar?"

"I'm sorry."

"Do you recognize the building in the background?" he asked.

She peered at it closely. "Boston University has several that look like this one. I'm afraid I can't be more specific."

His first guess had been a good one. "You're sure it's Boston U?"

"Yes," she said as she handed the photo back to him. "I'm sorry I can't be of more help."

Zach dug his business card out of his pocket. "If you happen to think of anything else, could you call me? We'll be in town for a few more days." He jotted the hotel name and his room number on the back. "I'd appreciate it."

She took the card. "Is Rose a relative of yours?"

He nodded slowly. "Yes, she is."

"I hope you find what you're looking for."

"I hope so, too."

The trail at the university grew hot as Leslie spotted the exact building on Bay State Road. But as Zach had suspected, no one there could identify the man, although one of the clerks suggested they look in the school yearbooks.

Standing in the college library, facing years' worth of annuals with thousands of student photos in each, the task seemed daunting.

"Where shall we begin?" she asked.

"We'll start with thirty-nine years ago and work backward," he decided.

"It certainly would have been easier if the lady at Rose's apartment building remembered where Rose had worked," Leslie mentioned as she blew dust off the top of one volume before she opened it.

"No kidding. At least she steered us in this direction."

And so began hours of comparing yearbook photos with the man standing beside Rose. For two days, Zach studied the images in the hopes that one would jump off the page at him. None did.

By the middle of their third day in the library, Zach's eyes ached. "I'm afraid that even if I saw his picture, I wouldn't recognize him. Studio photos don't always resemble candid snapshots."

Leslie turned the page. "We might get lucky."

He closed the book he'd finished. "I wonder how the boys are doing?"

"When you called last night, it sounded as if they were having a ball with your parents. I could hear them screaming and I wasn't even on the telephone."

Thinking of them, he smiled. "Yeah. My folks are going to be glad when I come home."

"What did you tell them about your trip?"

"I hope you don't mind, but I said that you were attending a medical conference and asked me to go along."

"Zach!" she exclaimed, horrified. "You didn't."

"I did. I wasn't ready to tell them the truth."

"No, but do you realize what they must be thinking?"

"Yeah." His grin was decidedly wicked. "And they'd be right, too. Do you mind?"

"No, but I'm sure they're wondering how you could go on an extended trip with a woman they haven't met."

"We'll change that as soon as we're home again," he said.

"We're scheduled to fly back tomorrow."

He didn't need the reminder. It only served to emphasize how much work they still had to do. For the first time since he'd begun this search, he began to question his motives.

His indecision must have appeared on his face because Leslie asked, "Do you want to change our flight and stay a few more days?"

He had one important reason to stay—to find the man in the photo—but he had two even more important reasons to go. "I came here to find my family, my roots," he said thoughtfully. "The more I sit here and think about it, I realize that my family is back in Nevada, where they've always been."

Leslie smiled and pointed to the photo. "What do you want to do about him?"

Zach stared at the snapshot. "Deep down, I have this uncanny sense that he's our biological father. From the way he's looking at Rose, he obviously loved her."

"I'm sure he did."

His dream began to pale in comparison with his obligations and responsibilities. "But I have two boys who are waiting for me."

"Yes, you do."

He drew a deep breath, formulating his plan even as he spoke. "I'll take out a personal ad in the newspaper asking for information about Rose. Maybe someone will see the name and remember something important."

"In the meantime?"

He rose and held out his hand. "We're going home."

She smiled. "I was hoping you'd say that."

"But first," he said, "we're going to blow this joint and enjoy ourselves. I'm ready to kick up my heels for a night on the town, aren't you?"

"You don't need to ask twice."

"Where would you like to go?"

"Near the water," Leslie said promptly. "It's sacrilegious for landlubbers like us to miss dipping our toes in the Atlantic Ocean."

"The wharf it is."

Although Leslie had visited San Diego's Sea World, she wanted to see the New England Aquarium. They toured it until closing time, then Zach took her to a seafood restaurant where they shared grilled tuna steak and cajun bluefish. Afterward, as the sun set, Leslie wanted to stroll along the waterfront and bask in the experience. Zach obliged.

It was an idyllic evening for Leslie. Hearing the water lap against the pier, listening to the seagulls call as they dove for their meal, smelling the tang of saltwater in the company of a man she loved—it was heaven.

"I don't know about you," he said at one point, long after night had fallen, "but I'd really like to go back to our hotel."

It was the perfect end to an unforgettable day. "I'm ready," she said, anticipating an evening alone with Zach. Such opportunities would be few and far between once they were back in Reno.

At first, their lovemaking was fierce and frantic, as if they couldn't deny themselves another moment.

"I love you, Leslie," Zach murmured against her neck as they lay wrapped in each other's arms, totally spent.

His declaration brought tears to her eyes. "I never thought I'd hear anyone say those words to me again," she said with a catch in her voice.

"You have now. And I know the boys will soon feel the same way."

"I'm not so sure about that," she said dryly. "Keith

is still afraid I'm going to boss them around, and Kenny doesn't know what to think.''

''They're smart kids. They'll see you're as wonderful as I think you are.'' With that, he kissed her again. As the night went on, their lovemaking lost its frantic note and took a more leisurely pace, like a constantly fed bonfire. Leslie treasured those hours, storing the memories for those nights when they would have to serve as her bed companions.

The next morning, she woke early and listened to Zach's steady heartbeat as he slept.

You should have told him, her little voice chided.

Perhaps, she answered silently, but this trip was a fantasy, and she didn't want reality to spoil it until absolutely necessary. The news could wait until they returned home. Then, she promised herself, she wouldn't hold anything back.

Tell him now, her conscience urged. *Once you're home, it will be harder to find the opportunity.*

She knew that. But she was afraid.

Do you trust him?

Yes, she decided, she did. If she trusted him, then there was no time like the present. They would leave in a few hours, and their other responsibilities and obligations would soon press in on them.

Zach stirred beside her. ''You're awake early,'' he said in his husky, morning voice.

''I couldn't sleep,'' she said. Then, hoping that his brain was still too foggy to take in everything she said, she began to tell him her story.

''Do you remember I told you that I had some things in my past that you didn't know about?''

He yawned. ''Yeah, I remember.''

''I'd like you to know what they are.''

"Now?" He sounded incredulous in spite of his sleepy state.

"Yeah. Otherwise, I'm afraid we'll get interrupted."

His hand closed over her breast. "You still might, darlin'," he teased.

She nudged his hand aside. "I can't think when you do that."

"I don't mind."

"Zach," she warned.

"Okay. Shoot."

She winced at the word, although she knew it was only a phrase. "I'm afraid I let you believe that a car crash took the lives of my husband and son. At least, that's what most people assume when I mention being a widow. I almost think it would have been easier to accept." She drew a breath. "Their deaths were gun-related."

Zach instantly became alert at the mention of guns. No wonder she'd grown so tense about the ones in his cabinet and had made the boys promise to leave them alone.

"My husband collected guns," she said in a faraway voice. "I never quite understood his fascination because he never went hunting. He didn't even go to the gun club range to fire them, but they were his hobby. He could tell you their history in minute detail, identify them in an instant and disassemble and assemble them in seconds flat. Michael was known as an expert on firearms, and a few of the local dealers would call him for consultations.

"He'd just purchased an antique revolver at a gun show, and I don't know the technical terms, but the moving parts were stuck and he thought they must be gummed from years of neglect. His project that day—it was a Saturday—was to get it in working order.

"I went to work early that morning, and I said what I always said whenever I knew he was going to drag out his cleaning supplies. 'Be careful.' I kissed him, then Brandon, and went to the hospital."

Zach hugged her, not sure if she even felt his presence as she relived that fateful day.

"I found out later that he'd started to clean the gun, but somehow, the mechanism jammed because there was a bullet still in the chamber. The gun accidentally fired. It killed our son, who was playing on the floor on his blanket."

She closed her eyes as if to dispel the images from her mind. Zach didn't think she was successful.

"My husband was distraught. He called nine-one-one to explain what had happened, but he went to pieces. The dispatcher tried to calm him down, but a minute later, she heard another gunshot."

"Oh, Leslie," he murmured.

"Before the police arrived, I came home from the hospital, not suspecting anything unusual. I walked into the house and found the two of them, lying next to each other. Blood was everywhere. The moment I saw them, I knew they were dead, but I tried CPR anyway. The police arrived a few minutes later, along with an ambulance."

Zach hardly knew what to say, except to murmur his condolences. It seemed such a trite thing to say how sorry he was, but he could find no other words to console her. "I'm so sorry for what you went through."

She nodded, but didn't speak.

"So you came to Reno to get away?" he asked, trying to direct her thoughts from that horrific scene.

"Eventually. There's an entire year in there where things are sort of a blur. This is the part I find hardest to tell, because a lot of people choose not to understand."

He tensed, wondering what would come next.

"I became so depressed that I couldn't function at home or at work. I lost my job because I didn't keep up with my paperwork. If that wasn't enough, my father passed away. I had no one left."

Zach couldn't imagine being so alone. When Zane's wife had died, the family had rallied around to support his brother. But in Zane's case, he *wanted* to be alone, which was part of his reason for jetting off to South America. If he ever returned, Zach would force him to talk to Leslie. Perhaps she could help Zane deal with his loss.

"At one point, I tried to wrap my car around a telephone pole," she continued. "While I was in the ER, my former boss intervened and told me how close I was to losing my medical license if I didn't get help. I didn't care about receiving treatment, but it took more energy to fight him than it did to go along with his suggestion, so I admitted myself to a private psychiatric clinic. Eventually I learned how to start living again.

"After I met you, I thought you deserved to know, but I couldn't make myself explain. I was afraid you might treat me differently and I didn't want to lose what we had."

"You wouldn't have then, and you aren't going to now," he said gently. "As for everyone else, they should understand after they hear your story."

"Not everyone is as open-minded as you are. Mention the word *psychiatric,* and they stop listening and start filling in the blanks."

"I hate to admit it, but you're right." An unrealistic urge to hunt down everyone who'd hurt her flooded over him.

"The hospital eventually reinstated me, but after a few months of my co-workers tiptoeing around me like I'd shatter, I had to leave. So I came to Reno."

He tightened his hold. "I'm glad you did. Does anyone at West View know the story?"

"My boss, Dr. Rice, does. One of the conditions of my employment is for him to oversee my work. And of course, the board of directors extended the length of my probation as a precaution."

"They can't do that without just cause," he said hotly, outraged on her behalf. "If you're doing your job—"

She ran her hand over his chest in a soothing motion. "I don't blame them. The reputation of their hospital could be at stake, not to mention the risk of lawsuits from people accusing me of incompetence. It seemed a small price to pay so I could practice medicine again. Besides, my probation won't last forever. Another month and it will be over."

"Does anyone else know?" he asked, thinking of the rumor his parents had brought to his attention.

"Dr. Rice's secretary, I suppose. She handles the paperwork."

Zach made a mental note to meet Dr. Rice and suggest that he plug the leak in his office.

"You're the only person I've told."

"I'm flattered."

He felt, rather than saw, her smile. "You shared your secret with me," she said softly, "so it only seemed fair to share mine with you, especially since we seem to be getting rather close."

Her fingers inched their way from his chest to his belly button and beyond. Immediately, his body stirred to life, and he quickly rolled her onto her back and covered her.

"We just *seem* to be getting close?" he repeated in a mock growl. "As far as I'm concerned, it's a sure thing. Shall I show you?"

"Please do," she breathed.

"YOU MUST HAVE had a good vacation," Betty said Monday morning. "Relaxing, was it?"

Leslie grinned. She was too happy to take offense at Betty's not-so-subtle inquisition. "Not really," she said. "We were always busy. Boston is filled with things to do."

Betty winked. "Was spending the day in a hotel room a part of your itinerary?"

"Now, Betty," Leslie responded, "haven't you heard that a woman never tells?"

The nurse laughed. "Yeah, but I never paid much attention to that advice. How else is a girl supposed to find out anything?"

"Ask your mother," Leslie said smartly.

"Yeah, right. But you did have a good time."

Leslie smiled, remembering. To think she'd been afraid to share her secret with Zach. He hadn't been appalled, only sympathetic, and for the first time since she left California, she felt as if she'd finally put that episode behind her. She'd truly been granted a second chance at happiness.

"The very best," she told her.

Betty thrust a chart in her hand. "I'm glad to hear it," she said heartily. "Now that you're rested and refreshed, I hope you brought your roller skates. You're going to need them.''

"You've been busy?"

"We would have to slow down to be called busy. Every day, we've beaten our record number of cases seen. There's hardly time to think. One of the guys has started a lottery for the day we'll hit our peak. If you want to sign up, see Mac. So far, there's fifty bucks to be won." She grinned. "You can take your sweetie pie to dinner.''

Leslie ignored her last comment. "What day did you choose?"

A technician stopped at the nurses' station. "Where's the fellow who needs the EKG?"

"Room five." While he scurried off in the right direction, Betty answered Leslie's question. "The middle of next month.''

"That bad?"

"It's spring," Betty said. "For some reason, we're seeing a lot of accident-prone people. Then there are the guys who've sat around all winter and gotten out of shape. Now they're doing too much and having heart attacks.''

"Lucky us.''

Betty tapped the chart on the counter. "Better get going. There's more where this one came from.''

Leslie's morning passed in organized chaos as she ordered tests, reviewed results and answered phone calls. Right before noon, she gratefully sent her last patient on his way. From her vantage point near the nurses' desk, she noticed a casually dressed man standing near the entrance with a camera slung around his neck and a stenographer's notepad in hand.

Leslie stopped Betty as he snapped several photos of the ER. "Who's the reporter?"

Betty shrugged. "Some guy with one of the local rumor rags. He's been hanging around the last few days, but he disappears whenever security shows up."

"I wonder what he's doing here? We haven't had any celebrities walk through the door."

Betty rolled her eyes. "He probably got a hot tip that we delivered a two-headed baby or some other such drivel."

Leslie sighed. ER was no place for nosy tabloid reporters. "Call security to get rid of him."

She headed toward her office, but before she could reach her private sanctum, the fellow appeared at her side. She started her you'll-have-to-leave speech, but he eyed her name tag and smiled.

"Dr. Hall? I'm Charlie Kellogg with the *Reno Review*. I'm doing a story about how hospitals are surviving in today's cost-conscious environment. Is it true that staff salaries are one of the largest drains to a facility's resources?"

"You'll have to talk to someone from our public information office," she said firmly, momentarily surprised by his intelligent question.

"I will, but surely you can spare a few minutes for me."

"No, I can't."

He flashed an engaging grin and continued as if she hadn't refused. "Is it accurate to say that West View is hiring unlicensed physicians in order to cut costs?"

"No."

His beady-eyed gaze seemed to pin her like a bug to a mounting board, and his smile took on a predatory smirk. "I understand that you're earning less than your colleagues in the same position."

"I wouldn't know. If you'll excuse me—"

He stepped in front of her, preventing her from crossing the threshold of her office. "Then you don't believe your lower salary is directly related to the loss of your license to practice medicine in California?"

CHAPTER FOURTEEN

LESLIE STOOD frozen, momentarily speechless. "You've been misinformed," she said in an icy tone.

"You're right. I apologize. It's more accurate to say that you lost your medical staff privileges. Isn't that correct?"

His voice carried over the noise of the department. Out of the corner of her eye, she saw several nurses stop in their tracks to exchange curious glances and listen with unabashed interest.

"No comment," she reiterated. "Now step aside."

"Why did you lose your privileges, Dr. Hall?" he pressed. "Did you misdiagnose a patient? Screw up a procedure?"

Leslie clenched her fists. "Betty, did you call security?"

Betty's eyes were huge. "They're on their way."

Obviously the threat of being escorted off the premises didn't faze Charlie in the slightest. He pressed on. "Was your stay in a private clinic a result of losing your job, and are you still under a psychiatrist's care? What's your relationship with Zachary Dumas?"

His questions flew at her like missiles, each landing with deadly accuracy. Escape became her only thought, but she had nowhere to go. Panic rose, but she knew she had to keep calm. No matter what she might say in her defense, the reporter would twist it to suit his needs. Sensationalism sold his tabloid, not the facts.

Suddenly, an authoritative voice interrupted. Her boss, Norman Rice, had arrived with two burly hospital security guards but Leslie felt more relief at the sight of the tall man walking alongside them. The whys and hows eluded her, but Zach was here, and at the moment, she needed his presence as never before.

"If you have questions pertaining to this hospital or our staff, you can direct them to me," Norman said firmly. "Otherwise, these officers will escort you to the nearest exit."

"My questions are for Dr. Hall."

"She isn't giving interviews," Norman replied. He exchanged glances with Zach before Zach ushered her into her office and closed the door.

"Oh, Zach," she groaned. "What's going to happen now? West View will get its name dragged through the mud and—"

"And Dr. Rice will take care of it," he assured her as he held her. "Don't worry."

"Don't worry?" she screeched. "Did you see everyone's faces?" Their expressions of shock, disbelief and dismay were indelibly etched on her mind. "How will I be able to work with them now?"

"Don't sell them short," he said. "Now that word is out, so to speak, be open and tell the truth. I'm sure you'll find the situation isn't as bad as you think."

She didn't have the same level of faith that he did, but one thing was certain—she couldn't hide any longer. If she wanted to hang on to the life she'd built, she had to switch her strategy from defensive to offensive. Her staff deserved to hear the truth from her own lips.

She inhaled a bracing breath. "All right. I'll do it."

"That's my girl," he said. "Remember, you won't be alone. I'll be right beside you." He kissed her lightly on the lips. "For luck."

She managed a smile before she stepped out of his embrace. Squaring her shoulders, she strode out of her office with purpose, not surprised to see the ER staff milling around the nurses' desk and wearing stunned expressions.

"You probably heard what the reporter said." At their collective nods, she continued. "Two years ago, my husband accidentally shot our son with a handgun. When he realized what he'd done, he couldn't face it and he killed himself. I found them when I came home from work one afternoon."

Someone gasped, but she didn't stop. "I couldn't deal with it, and my work suffered. I lost my staff privileges when I fell behind in my paperwork. To make a long story short, I was hospitalized for severe depression for six weeks at a private clinic. After months of therapy, I came to accept my loss and was able to go on. I needed a fresh start, so I chose West View because I had childhood ties in this area. If any of you feel my history affects your confidence in me practicing medicine, then I'd appreciate knowing now."

The formerly chaotic department became silent enough to hear a needle drop.

"Doesn't bother me what happened," a lanky young man announced with a shrug. "Personally, I think we all have to be a little crazy to work in this department. Even if we aren't, I've seen the way you move heaven and earth to save a life, Dr. Hall. If no one else wants to work on your shift, I will."

A chorus of *Me, too*s rang out. Leslie's eyes filled

with tears at their obvious support. "I doubt if Charlie Kellogg will show us in a good light," she warned.

"Who cares?" someone said. "Nobody believes the articles in his paper."

"You mean there really aren't space aliens buried in our cemetery?" another nurse asked with feigned disappointment.

"You're thinking of Roswell, not Reno," an intern responded.

The crowd tittered, and Leslie's mood rose like a helium balloon.

"Don't worry, Dr. Hall. If people ask about you, we'll tell them enough good stuff that they'll end up *begging* to come here when they're sick."

Leslie smiled through her tears, realizing that at some point, her hand had found its way into Zach's. "Thanks," she said.

Betty stepped forward. "Okay, people. The show is over. Back to work."

The group slowly dispersed, but not before several gave Leslie reassuring pats and comforting smiles. As the last few turned away, Leslie saw the guy she'd seen the night Zach had taught her to play pool. Immediately, she tensed.

Zach, apparently sensing the change that had come over her, took charge. "You're the man from the bar," he said.

The fellow nodded as he approached. "That was quite a touching story. Short, but succinct."

"What do you want?" Zach snarled.

"Vincent Buchanan, at your service," he said, extending his hand. "Call me Vince."

Leslie ignored his friendly gesture, as did Zach. "What do you want?"

"I wanted an interview, but it appears Charlie ruined my prospects."

"No kidding." Zach glared.

"All isn't lost, though. I got the information I came after. But before I go, I'd like to apologize. This wasn't the way I intended to get the information for my article."

Another reporter? "Oh, really?" Leslie asked, unconvinced.

"I'd heard a rumor about a lady doctor at West View and I started to investigate. Unfortunately, it appears as if Charlie has some of the same sources, which is troubling, I don't mind saying. Credibility issues, you know."

"What do you want?" Zach ground the words out.

Sensing Zach was about to do something he would regret in a cooler moment, Leslie placed a restraining hand on his arm. His tension eased at her smile, and she waited for Vince to explain.

"I was doing a piece on mental hospitals and how society's view of them has changed. Although not all patients become Pulitzer prizewinning mathematicians like John Nash, the public likes stories with happy endings. Your case falls in that category. Wouldn't you agree?"

Conscious of Zach's comforting presence, Leslie nodded. "I think so."

Vince grinned. "Anyway, good luck to you. Both of you."

Leslie watched his retreating figure, hardly able to deal with the speed at which the tables had turned. The question that had popped in her mind earlier burst forth.

"What brought you here with such perfect timing?"

Zach shifted his weight. "You know that rumor he

mentioned? Well, my parents had heard something similar, and they told me about it weeks ago.''

"Then you knew?" she asked, horrified. "Your parents, too? I can imagine what they must think of me."

"I told them it had to be a lie or a distortion of the truth. I totally disregarded it until you explained. I came today to inform your boss that his office had developed a leak and he'd better plug it. We'd just finished our conversation when we got the call about a nosy reporter."

She threaded her arm through his. "I'm glad you were here."

He patted her hand. "I am, too. Do you think you'll be all right?"

"Yes. I'm going back to work."

"Want me to stick around for a while? Take you to lunch? Hold your hand?"

She appreciated his thoughtfulness. "Holding my hand sounds nice, but I'll be fine."

"Drive out to the ranch after your shift," he said. "We'll celebrate with homemade ice cream."

"It's a deal."

"ARE YOU sick in your head, Dr. Hall?"

"Keith," Eleanor Dumas chided. "Where are your manners?"

"You always said if we don't know something, we should ask," Keith insisted. "So we're asking."

Keith had fired his question at Leslie the moment she'd walked through the door of their home and found Zach's entire family there, including his parents. It had been two weeks since "the incident," as she called it, and she assumed that the topic had died for lack of interest. Apparently not.

"Do you think I am?" she asked, stalling for time to prepare her explanation in terms that a ten-year-old would understand.

"No, but Grandma bought a newspaper at the grocery store with your picture on it. There was a big article, too, right next to the one about the half-wolf half-man."

"Mom," Zach demanded. "Why did you waste your money?"

"I had to know what the man wrote," Eleanor retorted. "If you want to fight fire, you have to know what's burning."

"It's all right," Leslie assured him. Obviously Norman hadn't been completely successful in squelching Charlie's story.

She faced the boys. "I had some trouble for a time in my life. Have you ever lost something or someone and knew you'd never see them again?"

"When our dog ran away," Keith said.

"When we moved away from Daddy," Kenny added.

"That wasn't the same," Keith insisted. "We knew we'd see him again."

"But it was a long time," Keith reminded his brother.

"Then you remember how that felt," Leslie said. As they nodded, she continued. "You knew you'd see your father again, but after my husband and baby died, I knew I'd never see them again. Ever."

"And that made you sad," Kenny broke in.

"Yes, it did. Have you ever been so unhappy that you wanted to stay in bed with the covers pulled over your head?"

Kenny nodded.

"That's how I felt. I didn't have a mother or a brother to talk to, so I went to a place where people listened to how I felt and they helped me straighten out my thoughts again.''

''So you wouldn't have to stay in bed with the covers pulled over your head?'' Kenny asked.

She smiled. ''That's right.''

''It was too bad you had to go to a place like that,'' Kenny said.

''It was, but I made new friends and now I'm okay.''

''Do you still miss your husband and baby?'' Keith asked.

''Every day,'' she told them. ''But when I meet people like you and your family, I don't feel quite so bad.''

''When my first hamster died, I got another one to take his place,'' Kenny said. ''Maybe you'll get another husband and baby.''

She laughed and tousled his short hair. ''It's not that easy, but someday I might. In the meantime, I'll just visit you.''

''Great.'' With the subject apparently explained to their satisfaction, the twins' attention turned to a more interesting topic. ''When are we going to start the popcorn, Grandpa?''

''As soon as we find the popper.''

''Okay,'' they chorused, then jostled each other to be first as they followed their grandfather into the kitchen.

Eleanor took Leslie's hands in hers. ''My dear,'' she said kindly. ''It's so nice to finally meet you. Zach explained everything before I even saw the paper. I'm sorry for your loss.''

''Thank you,'' Leslie said, touched by the woman's sincerity. Then again, Eleanor had endured her own struggles. ''Zach has told me so much about you.''

Eleanor's eyes sparkled with humor. ''Good things, I hope?''

"Absolutely."

"Grandma." Keith stood at the door. "We're ready for you *now*."

"They're impatient, so I'd better make sure they don't burn the kitchen down," Eleanor murmured. "I'm coming," she said as she headed in her grandson's direction.

"You handled that very well," Zach said. "I'm impressed."

"They need to understand," she said simply.

"I think they do," Zach said. "And moving on to happier thoughts, shall we see if any of that popcorn is ready for us?"

"I thought you'd never ask."

As soon as they joined Eleanor and Hamilton in the kitchen, Eleanor said, "You never have told us about your trip to Boston. Did you do any sight-seeing?"

Zach glanced at Leslie, and she shrugged ever so slightly in silent support of whatever he decided to tell them.

"Mom? Dad? You'd better sit down. There's something you should know."

Eleanor and Hamilton sat warily.

Keith nudged Kenny. "Ugh. This sounds like a grown-up talk."

"Yes, it is," Zach said, "so you two are excused. Take your popcorn and go to your room."

"But, Dad," they began in unison. "You said we're not supposed to eat in there."

"Then go outside."

Leslie watched the boys eagerly obey.

"What's this all about, son?" Hamilton asked.

"I have the most incredible story to tell you," Zach

answered. "Leslie? Would you find the box? It's by my bed."

Leslie knew exactly what he wanted. After a brief search, she found it resting on the bottom shelf of his nightstand.

When she returned, she saw that Eleanor's eyes were moist and Hamilton's face was wooden. Obviously, she'd missed most of the telling.

"It's incredible that Dr. Keller switched us," Zach said as he took his parents' hands in his. "But I'm so glad he did. I can't imagine growing up with anyone other than you."

Eleanor wiped her eyes. "Oh, Zach. After you came to us with your blood test results, I started thinking. I remembered how I felt the day I went into labor. I had this sense that something was wrong and I told your father about it."

She gazed at her husband. "He tried to convince me it was just new mother nerves, but I knew otherwise. Later, when Walter's nurse brought you to me, I thought Hamilton was right, and I wondered how I could have been so wrong.

"I asked Walter about my premonition later, and he simply smiled and said not to dwell on it because I had two sons who would require all of my time and attention. I took his advice. Over the years, I'd reflect about that day, but only long enough to be thankful for my boys."

"I wasn't going to tell you," Zach said with a suspicious hoarseness in his voice. "But someday, someone might come looking for us because of the inquiries Leslie and I made. I didn't want you to be shocked."

Hamilton nodded. "Are you going to keep searching?"

"We've done what we can, short of hiring an investigator, but I won't do that until I talk to Zane first. For the moment, I'm going to concentrate on the family I already have."

Leslie watched Zach clasp his father's aged hand in his work-roughened one. "Regardless of what any blood test shows, Zane and I are Dumases, through and through."

Hamilton's eyes also filled with a suspicious glint. "Don't you forget it," he said gruffly.

"I won't."

Eleanor rose. "Gracious sakes. This has been quite a day for all of us. I think we need some coffee."

"Regular or decaf?" Hamilton asked with curiosity.

"You're safe here, Dad," Zach said with a smile. "No decaf in this house."

Eleanor shook her head. "I suppose *one* cup won't hurt you. As for you, Zach, I'm counting on Leslie to mend your unhealthy ways."

"I'm afraid I won't be of much use in the coffee battle," Leslie admitted. "I prefer the regular kind myself."

Hamilton slapped his leg and guffawed. "You're outvoted, Ellie."

With the somber mood lightened, Leslie enjoyed herself with Zach's family for the next few hours. Later, after they'd cleared away their light dinner of Eleanor's homemade vegetable soup and sandwiches, the telephone in Zach's office rang. While he went to answer, Leslie intended to wheedle some of Zach's childhood stories from his parents. Before she could, Zach's voice drifted down the hall, as if the acoustics of his house seemed to funnel his comments directly at her.

"Now, Monica," he said, "since when do you believe those supermarket tabloids."

Instinctively, Leslie knew that she was the subject of Monica's call. Obviously, word—or a copy of the *Reno Review* itself—had somehow reached her in Seattle. Leslie should have started a conversation, but instead, she shamelessly eavesdropped.

"Yes, she was in a psychiatric clinic," she heard Zach say before a brief pause. "Monica, she'd just lost her husband, her baby and her father. How many people would bear up under that without needing help?

"She is not flaky like old man Kraus. She doesn't ramble or talk to herself, space out in the middle of a conversation or act homicidal.

"The boys are just getting settled in. You can't yank them out of here like yo-yos. Leslie isn't a bad influence and she won't hurt them. She's a doctor, for God's sake."

Leslie's heart sank to her toes. She didn't need to hear Monica's side of the conversation. It was painfully obvious what she thought. From the expression on Eleanor's face, she'd drawn the same conclusions.

"I'm not going to tell Leslie to stay away," Zach said. "Don't do this, Monica," he warned in his next breath. "You're not being fair or reasonable to demand the boys move back with you."

Leslie drew a tremulous breath as she stared at Eleanor, then at Hamilton. "He'll lose the boys and it will be my fault."

"Zach will talk sense into her," Eleanor advised, but Leslie saw the worry in her eyes, and her confidence shook to its foundation.

The boys burst into the kitchen for a drink, filling their glasses noisily from the tap. Leslie numbly watched their furtive attempt to sneak several cookies from the jar. She'd been foolish to believe that Zach's opinion was the only one that counted.

"I couldn't live with myself if he lost the boys," she said softly as she struggled to her feet. "He's talked about having them live here for nearly as long as I've known him. I won't be responsible for ruining his dream."

"Leslie, wait," Eleanor urged. "Don't go."

Leslie hesitated near the door and managed a weak smile as she took one last glimpse of the family she'd hoped to claim as hers. "I have to. Thanks for everything. Tell Zach…" What could she tell him? "Goodbye."

Within minutes, she roared down the road to Reno, trying to see through her tears. How many times could a person's heart break before it wouldn't heal?

ZACH TRIED to let Monica's ravings wash over him like water over a rock. It was easier said than done.

"How can I sleep at night knowing that my children could be in danger?" she complained.

"Crossing the street can be dangerous, Monica. Leslie is good with the boys, and they like her. She has the healthiest mental attitude of anyone I know."

His ex-wife scoffed. "I haven't done time in a funny farm, Zach."

"Your ignorance is showing, Monica," he said, hanging on to his temper. Aggravating her wouldn't help his cause. One of them had to be the voice of reason in this situation, and it obviously wouldn't be his ex-wife. He repeated a condensed version of the story he'd given his parents, then said, "Leslie went through hell and back, but she's more levelheaded than anyone you'll ever meet.''

"You're just saying that because you're obviously sleeping with her."

"Don't be ridiculous," he snapped. "If you don't want to take my word for it, call the hospital and talk to the chief of staff, Norman Rice. Better yet, talk to the people she works with on a daily basis."

"You've been taken in by a pretty face. If she wasn't unstable, why would the hospital keep such close tabs on her? I'm telling you, Zach, if she comes around the boys, I'm bringing them to Seattle."

"You can't uproot them again. They're just now starting to settle into a routine." He was starting to repeat himself—a sure sign to end a conversation that was going nowhere.

"I want to know my boys will be safe."

"In case you've forgotten, they're mine, too," he said. "I want them to be safe, as well, but if you're going to dictate the people I can associate with, then I assume I can do the same. What about the guy you dated who drank beer by the case? Or the fellow who landed in jail a few times for breaking and entering? And what about—"

"The men I see are my business."

"Yes, they are, but if you meddle in my life, then be prepared for a little meddling in yours, too. Turn about is fair play."

"Okay, okay. I get the picture."

"I'm not sure you do, Monica," he said. "Can you honestly say that if you came home and found Keith and Kenny dead on the floor, you would sail through the experience without any emotional problems whatsoever?"

There was silence.

"Well?" he demanded.

"I'll leave things as they are for now, but I won't promise they'll stay that way," she warned. "I'll drive up next weekend, and we'll decide what we're going to do. Until then, I don't want the boys around her. If they are, don't expect to see them past Saturday."

At least she hadn't insisted that he stick them on the first plane to Seattle. If this was a sampling of the sort of bigotry Leslie endured, he couldn't blame her for keeping the information to herself and wanting to start over.

"Leslie is here now. What do you want me to do? Tell her she can't talk to Keith and Kenny? Or should I send her home like a misbehaving child?"

"That's your problem. I told you how I feel, and if you go against my wishes, I'll have you in court so fast you won't know what hit you."

He heaved a silent sigh, hating the position she'd placed him in. "We'll see you on Saturday."

Zach returned to the kitchen, frustrated. "Monica is being difficult," he told his mother. "Totally unreasonable."

"What did she say?"

"She doesn't want Leslie around the boys. She's coming this weekend to reevaluate her decision to let them stay with me. I had no idea she was so narrow-minded, but she'll have to get over it." He glanced around the room. "Where's Leslie?"

"She left, Dad," Keith said.

"Did she get called back to the hospital?"

The glimmer in his mother's eyes warned him of impending bad news. "She overheard your part of the conversation and filled in the blanks."

"She knows that Mom doesn't want her around us," Keith added.

"Is that true?" he asked his mother.

"I'm afraid so, son."

"Didn't you tell Mom that Leslie was really nice?" Kenny asked.

"Sometimes your mother doesn't listen." He began to pace, furious at his ex-wife, furious at himself for not closing the door. "I'm not going to let Monica do this."

"For the time being, you don't have much choice," Eleanor said softly. "She is the custodial parent, and until that's changed, she can do what she wants."

"She always did want me to dance to her tune," he said bitterly.

"Leslie knows that, which is why she went home. She didn't want to go, but she doesn't want you to lose the boys. It was a generous thing for her to walk away— a completely selfless decision on her part. She must really love you."

He knew she did, and he knew that having lost her family, she wanted him to have his. Leslie would always do what she thought was the right thing, even if it cost her dearly.

"I love her, too, Mom. I want her in my life as much as I want Keith and Kenny."

"I know, Zach. Be patient. Things will work out."

At times and under the right conditions, he possessed the patience of Job. With situations where logic had flown the coop, like the one affecting him now, he had none. Frustration gnawed at him as he imagined the rejection Leslie must be feeling. The relationship he'd envisioned with her didn't include splitting his life into two distinct parts—one with the boys and one with Leslie. Monica's interference made reconciling the two so they would overlap a formidable, and nearly impossible, task.

ON SATURDAY, Leslie walked out of a last-minute ER staff meeting with Betty. It was almost three, and although her shift would end in an hour, she wasn't looking forward to another long, lonely night ahead.

"Some of us are trying out a new Mexican restaurant tonight," Betty said. "Why don't you come with us?"

It had been five days since Leslie had left Zach's ranch, five days since she'd lost her appetite, five days since she'd stored her coffeepot in the back of a cabinet. Hearing the word *Mexican* brought Armando's and her memories of that evening with Zach to mind. "I'm not hungry."

"We're not going until seven."

"I'll think about it."

Betty's gaze grew sympathetic. "I know it's been tough on you, but cheer up. That Vince fellow's article in the newspaper was wonderful. Maybe Zach's ex-wife will see it and have a change of heart."

"And maybe we'll receive twenty percent raises this year."

"It's possible," Betty insisted.

"But highly unlikely." Leslie smiled at the nurse. "Go on and enjoy what you can of the weekend."

"What are you going to do?"

"I'm going to finish piecing my quilt top together."

"Bor-ing. Do you know what you need?"

"I have a feeling you're going to tell me."

"That's because I'm an expert at handing out advice. After we eat, we're going to this little tavern on the east side. It'll be more fun than sewing at home."

Leslie intended to refuse, then stopped. Forgetting

Zach would certainly be easier if she found something to take his place. A night out, surrounded by friends, seemed like a step in the right direction. It was rather sweet the way her staff had become so protective of her. They were all good people, and she wanted them to know she appreciated their efforts.

"I'll go," Leslie said.

"Great! Would you mind driving? In case I meet an interesting character who'll give me a ride home?" Betty winked.

"Sure." By bringing her car, she could leave whenever she wanted.

The ward clerk waved frantically at Betty. "Gotta run," she said.

"I'm going to radiology if you need me," Leslie called after her.

Betty gave her a thumbs-up sign while Leslie went to the department next door to review an X ray. When she returned, Betty stood at the nurses' station, scribbling on a clipboard.

"Anything for me?" Leslie asked.

"Yeah. There's a guy in room two with chest pain."

"Is that his chart?"

"No, this is someone else's." Betty glanced around. "I guess I left it in his room. Gosh, I'd lose my head today if it wasn't attached."

"Did you order an EKG?"

"As we speak." She made a shooing motion. "Would you please go and do your job so I can do mine?"

Working with Betty had done more to shake her out of her doldrums than anything Leslie could imagine. "What happened to respect for physicians?" she teased.

"That went out with bell-bottoms. Now hurry up before the guy thinks we've deserted him."

Leslie opened the door to room three. "I'm Dr. Hall…" Her voice died as she saw Zach sitting on the edge of the bed. "Zach! What's wrong? You're having chest pains?"

He rose, his expression serious. "I am."

Worry had her dragging out her stethoscope to listen to his heart. "Are you—"

"I miss you, Leslie."

The steady beat told the tale. His complaint was just a ploy, a bid for her attention. "You're not ill, are you."

"Physically, no. In here, though—" he tapped the region over his heart "—I am."

"Oh, Zach. You shouldn't have come," she said miserably as she stuffed her equipment into her pocket.

"You wouldn't return my phone calls," he reminded her. "I had to come in person. Betty suggested this was the best way to make sure you listened to me."

"You can't pretend to be a patient every time you want to talk," she told him. "Monica will cause problems, no matter what we do."

"She only said that she didn't want you near the boys. She didn't say a word about me seeing you."

"She doesn't have to. In the end, you'll pay the price."

He shook his head. "We've worked out everything. The twins are staying with me. Monica was going to drive up this weekend to discuss the situation, but she had a change of heart."

"She did?" His news overwhelmed her, and she sank onto the bed. "How?"

"Between the copies of the article our friend Vince wrote, and my reminder that if she wants to choose my friends then she won't mind if I afford her the same privilege, she admitted that she might have overreacted.''

Leslie couldn't believe it. His assurances were a dream come true, but since some of her dreams had turned into nightmares, she wasn't willing to embrace this good news just yet.

''Then she really doesn't mind if I spend time with the boys?''

His mouth twisted into a wry smile. ''She's holding me personally responsible for their safety. I figure once a few weeks go by, she'll forget the whole thing. It doesn't hurt that Keith and Kenny have thrown their support in your direction.''

''They have?''

''Kenny wants you to come along on our fishing trips, and Keith has asked for your spaghetti salad again. Mom would also like you to help us plant bushes in Rose and Isaac's honor.''

''Isaac?''

''That was the name they'd chosen for their baby. When they realized they had two to name instead of one, they picked Zachary and Zane.''

''I'd be honored to help.'' She hesitated. ''Then it's really okay?'' Maybe if she repeated it often enough, the fact would soak into her brain.

''It's really okay,'' he echoed as he lifted a flat package off the bed and handed it to her. ''Open it.''

She tore off the brown paper and nearly gasped at the framed sketch of her seated on his porch swing, staring into the distance. ''When did you draw it?'' she asked.

''Over the past few days,'' he said. ''I carried this

picture of you in my head. It's from the night we barbecued."

Tears welled in her eyes. "It's beautiful."

He pulled her to her feet to stand in his embrace. "Marry me, Leslie, and share my family with me."

"Aren't you moving a little fast?" she asked, feeling her cloud of despair disappear. "Until a few minutes ago, we weren't able to see each other."

"If you don't want to set a date, we won't. I just need to know that you're mine."

How could she possibly refuse the love of her life? "I am," she promised, making a mental note to restore her coffeepot to its place on the counter. "Nothing could make me happier than to become your wife."

"So when can we make it happen?"

She smiled at his impatience. "When everyone is used to the idea."

"They'll get used to the idea after we're married."

She shook her head. "You can't have a wedding without your brother."

"We could be waiting a long time," he complained.

"You can handle it."

"Are you always going to argue with my suggestions?" he grumbled good-naturedly.

"It depends," she said primly. "Now, if you ever have the urge to kiss me, I won't object."

"Say no more."

As Zach's arms came around her and his mouth descended to meet hers, he delighted in his good fortune. He might never know the identity of his birth father, but in searching for him, Zach had discovered something far greater.

He'd found a love to last a lifetime.

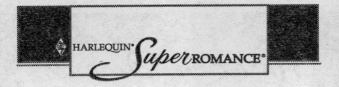

HARLEQUIN *Super*ROMANCE®

...there's more to the story!

Superromance.
A *big* satisfying read about unforgettable
characters. Each month we offer *six* very different
stories that range from family drama to adventure
and mystery, from highly emotional stories to
romantic comedies—and much more! Stories
about people you'll believe in and care about.
Stories too compelling to put down....

Our authors are among today's *best* romance
writers. You'll find familiar names and talented
newcomers. Many of them are award winners—
and you'll see why!

If you want the biggest and best
in romance fiction, you'll get it
from Superromance!

Emotional, Exciting, Unexpected...

HARLEQUIN®
Makes any time special ®

Visit us at www.eHarlequin.com

HSDIR1

HARLEQUIN®
INTRIGUE

WE'LL LEAVE YOU BREATHLESS!

If you've been looking for thrilling tales of contemporary passion and sensuous love stories with taut, edge-of-the-seat suspense—then you'll love Harlequin Intrigue!

Every month, you'll meet four new heroes who are guaranteed to make your spine tingle and your pulse pound. With them you'll enter into the exciting world of Harlequin Intrigue— where your life is on the line and so is your heart!

THAT'S INTRIGUE— ROMANTIC SUSPENSE AT ITS BEST!

HARLEQUIN®
Makes any time special ®

Harlequin® Historical

From rugged lawmen and valiant knights to defiant heiresses and spirited frontierswomen, Harlequin Historicals will capture your imagination with their dramatic scope, passion and adventure.

*Harlequin Historicals...
they're too good to miss!*

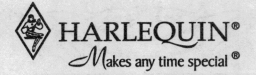

HARLEQUIN®
Makes any time special ®

AMERICAN *Romance*

Upbeat, All-American Romances

HARLEQUIN®
Duets™

Romantic Comedy

Harlequin®
Historical

Historical, Romantic Adventure

HARLEQUIN®
INTRIGUE

Romantic Suspense

Harlequin Romance ®

Capturing the World You Dream Of

HARLEQUIN® *Presents*

Seduction and passion guaranteed

HARLEQUIN® *Super* ROMANCE®

Emotional, Exciting, Unexpected

HARLEQUIN®
Temptation.

Sassy, Sexy, Seductive!

HDIR1

HARLEQUIN®
Makes any time special ®

 Upbeat,
All-American Romances

HARLEQUIN®
Duets™ Romantic Comedy

Harlequin® Historical Historical,
Romantic Adventure

HARLEQUIN®
INTRIGUE Romantic Suspense

Harlequin Romance ® Capturing the World
You Dream Of

HARLEQUIN® *Presents* Seduction and passion
guaranteed

HARLEQUIN® *Super* ROMANCE® Emotional,
Exciting, Unexpected

HARLEQUIN® *Temptation* Sassy, Sexy, Seductive!

magazine

❤ ────────────────────────────── **quizzes**

Is he the one? What kind of lover are you? Visit the **Quizzes** area to find out!

❤ ───────────────────── **recipes for romance**

Get scrumptious meal ideas with our **Recipes for Romance.**

❤ ──────────────────────── **romantic movies**

Peek at the **Romantic Movies** area to find Top 10 Flicks about First Love, ten Supersexy Movies, and more.

❤ ────────────────────────── **royal romance**

Get the latest scoop on your favorite royals in **Royal Romance.**

❤ ──────────────────────────────── **games**

Check out the **Games** pages to find a ton of interactive romantic fun!

❤ ──────────────────────── **romantic travel**

In need of a romantic rendezvous? Visit the **Romantic Travel** section for articles and guides.

❤ ────────────────────────────── **lovescopes**

Are you two compatible? Click your way to the **Lovescopes** area to find out now!

 HARLEQUIN® ❤

makes any time special—online...

Visit us online at
www.eHarlequin.com

HINTMAG